Trouble on Black Creek

By
Matt Buche

Trouble on Black Creek

Copyright © 2012 by Matt Buche

Artwork by Sharon Merchant

Cover design by Abbie Smith

Layout by Kait Lamphere

The opinions expressed in this manuscript are solely the opinions of the author and do not represent the opinions or thoughts of the publisher. The author represents and warrants that s/he either owns or has the legal right to publish all material in this book.

ISBN-13: 978-1-937580-38-4

First published in 2012

10 9 8 7 6 5 4 3 2 1

Published by   2 MOON PRESS
123 W. Michigan Ave, Marshall, Michigan 49068
www.800publishing.com

All Rights Reserved. This book may not be reproduced, transmitted, or stored in whole or in part by any means, including graphic, electronic, or mechanical without the express written consent of the publisher except in the case of brief quotations embodied in critical articles and reviews.

PRINTED IN THE UNITED STATES OF AMERICA

To my family and friends...
all that really matters

Chapter 1

Jim Parker was already awake when the first rays of sunlight crept across his bedroom floor. It had been a long night and sleep was not much a part of it. He lay there a while longer listening to the voices of his parents and savoring the moment.

His father was leaving for four months to work construction in Florida. It had been a slow year here in southern Michigan, but according to his Uncle Lou, who lived in Orlando, there was more work than he had men for. So in order to expand his business, he had called on Jim's dad, Ray, to come down and run his new crew. "Just long enough to earn enough money to get us through the winter," his dad said, "and hopefully start our own construction business back here next spring." At least that was the way he had worded it to his mother.

Jim knew she was not really keen on the idea, not only because she didn't want him to be gone that long, but because she wasn't very fond of Uncle Lou. His mother spoke her mind when the need arose. It was this sure-of-herself attitude that seemed to bother his uncle and had caused them to have words on more than one occasion. Nothing serious, just enough to cause his uncle's face to redden and storm off for a few days at a time. But that was several years ago, before he headed down south.

His dad looked up from his cup of coffee as Jim entered the kitchen and headed for the refrigerator. Jim didn't want to look at his father just yet.

"You got any questions about the chores or anything else before I take off, Son?"

"No, I guess I got everything straight," Jim answered nonchalantly.

Ray Parker had known the answer before he had asked. Jim had been doing most of the work around the place these past summer months anyway. Ray had been working up in Flint this whole summer, driving back and forth each day and had put most of the work on young Jim. He was proud of the boy, only fifteen, but already more responsible than many men twice his age.

"Well, if anything comes up, you just give Doc Anderson a call, especially if any of those last six sows have any trouble farrowing." Jim nodded and gave his mother a quick look as she flipped the last pancake off the hot griddle and onto a plate already overflowing. She offered a weak smile and motioned for him to sit down next to his father.

The talk over breakfast was awkward, but no one wanted it to end. Finally, his father stood up, walked to the kitchen window, and stared silently for a minute.

"I want you both to know this will be just as hard on me as it will be on you." Jim stared into his plate and fought to hold back the tears. His mother, however, could no longer contain herself and buried her face into her hands. Jim, not wanting to face the moment any longer, rose and walked into the back yard and tried to regain control over his emotions. Not that he felt shame for wanting to cry, but he knew his father was depending on him to look after things and it was time to face up to that responsibility.

Jim heard Max Logan's pickup coming up the drive long before he blew the horn. Their driveway was almost an eighth of a mile long, angling up off the dead end of Pratt Lake Road. A narrow trail ran from the turnaround at the dead end down to a crude boat landing in the cattails. Their farm overlooked the east end of Pratt Lake, which was straight north from their back yard. To the west the land broke down towards the swamp that bordered the south side of the lake, and to the south of the swamp were nearly a hundred acres of oaks, beech and maple that ran back to the east and bordered the south side of their eighty acres. Jim loved this place but even its beauty paled in the sadness he felt at the sound of Max's Ford pickup.

Looking back through the screen door into the kitchen, he saw his father and mother in each other's arms. Jim walked around the house to meet Mr. Logan just getting out of his truck.

"Hello, Jim. How're you doin'?"

"Fine, Mr. Logan. That boar you brought over sure did the job. Those first three sows he bred had thirteen or fourteen little ones apiece."

Max grinned. "Well, you just let me know next spring when you're ready for him again, and I'll bring him right over." Their conversation was cut short by the squeaking of the front porch door as his father came out of the house carrying his suitcase and work belt. His mother followed closely behind, her arms folded across her chest.

"Good morning, Max," she said, smiling politely.

"Morning, Ann," Max replied and stepped up to meet Ray. "I'll take these and wait for you in the truck." Jim stared down at the ground.

"I'll be home for Christmas and your cherry cobbler, Ann," Ray said smiling.

"And pork roast with mashed potatoes and gravy," she replied, smiling back weakly.

Ray stepped down off the porch and walked to Jim, putting an arm around his shoulder while still walking towards Max's truck. "I'll need you to look after your mom while I'm gone, Son." Ray was speaking softly now. "One more thing, keep your eye out for that Jubal Hayes." Jim felt his stomach turn. "I don't want to worry you, but that snake in the grass isn't above trying to make off with some of those hogs and anything else he can get his hands on."

Jim nodded his hands buried in his pants pockets.

His dad smiled, offering his hand. "See if you can bag that old buck hanging out down in Jackson Swamp." For the first time that day, a smile came to Jim's face.

"It's a deal," he said, grasping his father's hand. The two stood silently for a second, letting the moment linger. Finally, with a quick wave, and one last smile for the both of them, Ray Parker headed out the drive towards the train station and from there, a long ride to Florida.

Jim turned and headed toward the barn. Even though it was Saturday, he had lots of work to do, fences to check, pens to clean, and a trip to town for feed. School started Monday and he wanted as much of the farm work done as possible before then. He glanced back towards the house as he entered the barn and saw his mother still standing on the top step, arms folded, staring towards the slowly settling dust in the morning light.

Chapter 2

The bell sounding brought Jim back to reality. Even though Biology was his favorite subject, he had drifted off-daydreaming about hunting again. Bow season started in less than a month and even with all his extra work, he still couldn't wait. He scooped up his books, hurried out the door, and spotted his mother sitting in the truck out front. His mother's job at DeBoor's Grocery gave him both a ride to and from school. She only worked thirty hours a week, hours that coincided with Jim's hours at school.

Ann watched her son race down the front steps of the school, a smile crossing her face. She was glad school came easily for Jim. He reminded her of her father: smart, easy going, a man with a great love for the outdoors. A mother couldn't ask for a better son. The only worry she had for him was whether they would be able to afford college.

Jim threw his backpack into the truck bed and climbed in next to his mother. "Mom, can we stop at the Co-op on the way home?"

"I guess we can, why?" Ann said as she steered the truck onto 2nd Avenue and out towards the edge of town.

"Well, if we can pick up the feed this afternoon, it will save me a trip in the morning with the tractor and wagon."

"Okay," Ann said. Jim had worked hard all this week, up at six a.m. to do chores before school, then chores after school and homework after dinner. She was more than happy to make things a little easier for him. Besides, the elevator was right on their way out of town.

Elmdale was a typical southern Michigan farming community. The railroad ran through the heart of town with the Farmers' Co-op built alongside the tracks on the east side. On the other side of town and on the opposite side of the tracks were the Livestock Auction barns. The north side of town was bordered by the fertilizer plant and on the south Thompson's Farm Equipment Sales and Service. No matter which way a person came into the sleepy little village of five hundred, it was obvious that farming remained the backbone that held the town together.

Ann steered the old Ford into the parking lot of the Co-op elevator and backed it up to the loading dock. As Jim and his mother entered the office, Stan Porter, the manager, greeted them. Stan called out, "Afternoon, Ann, Jim. What can I do for you two today?"

"Well," Ann said, "Jim wanted to stop by and get this week's feed today, rather than come in tomorrow morning," replied Ann.

"Fine, I'll write your order up," Stan replied.

On the other side of the office, Jim walked up and down the aisles of farm supplies: boots, gloves, milking supplies, feed troughs, heat lamps, various medicines and ointments. Forks, shovels, hoes, and rakes lined the walls. Along another wall were salt blocks, bags of pig starter pellets, and calf milk replacer.

On the back wall, there were rows of coveralls, Carhart jackets, work shirts, pants and hats. Anything you could possibly need on the farm aside from a vet was available at the Co-op.

"See anything you need, Jim?" Stan asked, without glancing up from writing.

"Not right now, but I'll need some more pig starter pellets in a few weeks when I wean those first litters."

"Say, Ann," Stan said suddenly. "You know the Larson boy that works here on Saturday mornings?"

"You mean Art and Freda's boy, Tom?" Ann replied.

"That's him. Tomorrow's his last day. He's playing football this fall and says he wants his Saturdays free, so we'll need someone to replace him. Think Jim would be interested? It's only from eight to one each Saturday."

Jim popped his head out from behind a stack of pails. "Can I, Mom? I promise I'll keep up with my chores at home." He didn't bother to hide his excitement.

"Well, I guess it would be all right," Ann said.

"It would only be until the first of November," Stan said. "I promised Tom he could have his job back after football season. Would that still be all right with you, Jim?"

"Sure, that'll work out great." Jim walked up to the counter. "I start fox trapping around November first anyway."

"Start next Saturday," Stan said. He finished writing up the feed order. Ann asked him to put it on their account and took the receipt out to the mill.

"See you next Saturday at eight, Mr. Porter," Jim said as they headed out the door.

The feed was bagged, loaded on the truck and they were on their way out of town towards home in no time. Jim was already thinking how lucky he was. With his dad gone and money tight, he had been wondering where he could come up with a few dollars. He needed some new traps, lure, and a few new arrows. With a job, he wouldn't have to ask his mom and maybe even have enough left over for a new pair of waders. He had wanted to trap that stretch of Black Creek that wound its way through

Jackson's Swamp. The water there was too deep for his old hip boots.

Jim smiled. He was getting a little ahead of himself. He hadn't been to his first day of work and he already had his first check spent.

Ann turned the truck off the highway onto the dirt road that wound its way through the hardwoods that lined the road on both sides. Finally, the road started its slow descent down the hill overlooking Jackson's Swamp and then crossed over Black Creek, which divided the swamp in two. From there it climbed back up another hill on the other side, only to drop once again and finally dead end at Pratt Lake and their driveway.

Other than a few duck hunters, the road got very little use. Everyone had quit fishing the lake once the rumor had gotten around that the fish had all been frozen out a few years back.

Jim knew that rumor was not entirely true. Only a handful of people knew that the muck bottom in the lake had some fairly deep holes. Jim didn't mind people believing the rumor and he did nothing to convince them otherwise. Both he and his dad liked the privacy, and so they just let people go on believing the story.

Ann backed the truck up to the barn door. "I'll go start supper while you start chores. We'll eat a little early tonight."

Jim let the tailgate down on the truck and grabbed the first bag of feed to carry inside. "Good," he said. "I wanted to go back by that stand of clover before dark and see if I could spot that buck." He tossed the bag up on his shoulder and headed into the barn.

Jim unloaded the rest of the feed and then fed the six sows that had already had their litters. Each sow was in a separate pen with a hanging heat lamp for each litter. Wired into the corner of each pen was a metal trough for feed and water. A separate rubber trough was nailed against the opposite corner and was filled each day with starter pellets for the piglets.

Opposite the pens were six farrowing crates that held the six sows that hadn't given birth yet. The crates kept the sows' movement to a minimum in order to keep them from injuring the newborn pigs, either from stepping or laying on them.

After all the pigs in the barn were fed, Jim headed out back and fed the ten hogs in the lot out behind the barn. These pigs were near market weight and would soon be sold. They only fed a few pigs out all the way to market weight as the twenty-five acres of corn they raised each year could only supply so much feed. Instead, most of the pigs were sold as feeder pigs when they were around fifty pounds.

His chores done, Jim stuck his head inside the kitchen door. "How long 'til supper, Mom?"

"About twenty minutes," Ann replied as she dropped another peeled potato into the pot on the stove.

"OK, I'll be out back shooting my bow," Jim said.

Inside the garage attached to the old farmhouse, Jim lifted his recurve off the two nails on which it rested. He slipped the string over one end, then stepped through the string with his right leg and placed the end of the limb across his left foot. He pulled the upright limb forward, and slipped the string into place. The quiver attached to the bow held three arrows already, but these were tipped with broadheads, not the target points he wanted now, so he grabbed three more arrows off the shelf next to where he kept his bow. Still, he kept the hunting arrows in the quiver so that while he practiced the bow would be the same weight as when he was hunting. Shooting the bow without the arrows would make it shoot differently.

The target in the backyard was nothing more than three bales of straw stacked one on top of another and wrapped in black landscape plastic. On each end, a steel fence post was driven into the ground to help support them. Then from the top of each fence post ran a heavy string that supported a plastic feed sack packed with scrap plastic wrap his mother had brought home from work. The sack hung up off the ground in front of the bales. It was approximately the size of a deer's body with a small circle drawn towards one end to simulate a deer's vitals.

Standing about fifteen yards away, Jim placed the armguard on his left forearm and then slipped the finger tabs on his right hand. He nocked an arrow, took a deep breath and tried to relax.

His grandfather's words echoed in his head. Shooting a recurve is much like throwing a baseball. It's all hand-eye coordination and concentration; pick a spot, concentrate, then draw and release, all the while maintaining form and concentration well after the arrow has left the bow.

Jim drew, holding only for a second at full draw before releasing the arrow. *Thwap.* The arrow struck right on line but slightly high. Placing another arrow on the string, Jim narrowed his spot down even farther. Picking out a small piece of plastic dangling within the circle, he drew and released. The arrow sailed dead center within the circle.

Repeatedly, he sent the arrows toward the target. Most times they flew true, but every once in a while one would miss the mark. Each time that happened, Jim could figure out what had gone wrong. Usually he had taken his eye off his spot or maybe had made a poor release.

Jim was always amazed by the power contained in the limbs of a bow, just a simple stick and string, yet great concentration and practice were required to master such a simple device.

His grandfather had bought the bow at a garage sale when Jim was twelve. It was a Shakespeare Wonder Bow, 45 pounds draw weight at 27 inches. He had outgrown the bow last year, but really couldn't afford a new one. Besides that, since his grandfather had passed away a year ago this November, it had become more than just a bow.

Ann watched through the screen on the back door. She smiled at the serious look on Jim's face while the breeze tossed his black hair back and forth. Another year and he would be as tall as his father was. She thought about her father and how much he and Jim had meant to each other. She blinked away the moisture she felt gathering in her eyes and hollered out to Jim that supper was ready.

Chapter 3

Jim pushed his chair back from the table and patted his stomach. "Nothin' like pork chops and boiled potatoes," he said with a satisfied smile.

"There's still one pork chop left," Ann said.

"No thanks, I'm stuffed."

"I'll save it for breakfast with your eggs," Ann said.

"Steak and eggs for breakfast, you'd think we were rich," Jim joked as he got up from the table.

"Well, Mister Rich Farmer, we're about out of pork in the freezer, and it'll be a while longer before any of those hogs out back are ready to butcher. So you had better keep practicing with that bow of yours if you want to keep eating like this," Ann said, smiling.

"Since Dad won't be here for hunting season, you think I could go ahead and buy a second bow tag this year?" Jim asked.

"Don't you think you should wait until you've filled the first tag before you buy a second one?" Ann said.

In the past, Jim and his dad would buy one license apiece because they figured that two deer were all they could eat anyway.

Jim hunted with the bow because you could start bow hunting at twelve years old, you had to wait until fourteen to hunt with the gun. After he had bagged a doe that first year, he was hooked on bow hunting. His dad hunted with the gun only, not sharing Jim's interest in archery.

"I guess you're right." Jim grinned at his mother. "One for the freezer and then I'm going after that big boy down in Jackson's Swamp," he said.

Ann shook her head. "Talk like that and you'll end up with no deer at all."

"Well, I'm going to head down by the swamp and that stand of clover and see if that big buck shows himself tonight. Haven't seen him in a couple of weeks. I hope somebody didn't pick him off at night with a spotlight," Jim said.

"That big buck is all you and your dad have talked about all summer," Ann said as she began clearing away the dishes. "Just be back right after dark. I don't need to be worrying about you, too," she said, no longer kidding around.

Jim stepped out into the garage and grabbed his camouflage hat and jacket off the row of work clothes hanging along the wall. He stepped into his knee-high rubber boots that he kept just for hunting and fox trapping. They would leave behind no human scent wherever he walked.

As he headed out the door, he stopped and stepped back inside. Reaching under his dad's hunting jacket, he pulled out an old, worn set of binoculars. They had been his grandfather's, brought home from World War II, German made and, in their day, some of the finest.

Jim cut around behind the garage and headed towards the swamp along the south side of the lake and the north side of their property. They had twenty-five acres of corn that ran right along the swamp. At the west end of the corn fields, before the hardwood, were three acres of clover.

Jim and his dad had started it this spring. His grandfather had always talked about doing it for the deer, so after he had died last fall, Jim and his dad had worked up the three acres. Then, since it was too late in the year, they had to wait until this spring to drill the seed.

Sneaking along the edge of the corn and swamp, Jim was alert to any fresh deer sign along the way. There were deer tracks everywhere and an occasional rub on the willows. No rubs of any size, though there usually wasn't much buck sign this early anyway.

The willows were about seventy-five yards wide and ran the length of the field before giving way to a large stand of elm that stood at the north end of the hardwoods.

On the other side of the willows from this corn were the cattails that surrounded the lake. They were over five feet high and nearly one hundred yards wide before the actual lake began. It was no place to try to penetrate, and Jim knew that from experience.

Four years ago, he had tried to find a way through, looking for places to set some coon traps. What a nightmare. He ended up losing one of his boots and had to crawl out of the mucky mess. He smiled, thinking about the look on his mother's face when he had come through the back door, covered from head to toe with mud.

With the breeze blowing straight into his face, Jim had no worry of being scented. He still moved slowly, though, because with this much cover around him, he could be closer to deer than he realized.

As he neared the end of the corn, he could see out into the clover through the stalks of corn. A doe and two fawns were already feeding. Jim sneaked in about twenty rows over, staying about fifty yards from the edge of the clover.

He sat down on a small knoll, pulled the binoculars out of his coat pocket, and began glassing over the field.

The doe and two fawns were near the center of the clover. The old doe would take a few bites then quickly bring her head up and look around.

No other deer were on the field yet, so for the next ten minutes Jim occupied himself with watching the antics of the fawns as they ran back and forth chasing one another, jumping in the air, and pestering the old doe to no end.

Through it all, the old doe remained vigilant, always on the watch for danger. It was through her that Jim noticed the arrival of two more deer: the constant staring by the older doe in the direction of the hardwoods was soon followed by the appearance of another doe and fawn.

This doe was smaller, probably last year's fawn with her first offspring. They entered the field with no hesitation and began feeding alongside the others.

Jim thought more than likely the old doe was this younger doe's mother as well. Groups of does tended to be related and would stay together loosely as a family unit.

The young bucks, however, would move off or be driven off by the doe, usually in the fall. During that time of year, when the buck's testosterone level had began to rise, even the button bucks, became aggressive. It usually didn't take long for Ma deer to tell junior to pack his bags and move out.

The young bucks would usually stay in the area for the next year or so, keeping loose ties with the doe. However, come the next fall, when they were a year-and-a-half old and ready for their first breeding season, these young bucks would tend to wander. Perhaps only a half mile, but maybe as much as three miles- usually just far enough away to find an area where they could establish some dominance over other bucks in the area or where they were tolerated by the other bucks.

This time of year though, the bucks would still be in their bachelor groups. All summer long, the bucks would stay together, grow fat on the abundant food, and lounge away the hot summer days. Jim had seen as many as nine bucks together in one group. Usually, though, it would be smaller groups, three or four, maybe five.

It was a group such as this that Jim had been watching all summer. Four bucks altogether. Two year-and-a-half old bucks, both six-points, that appeared to be twins, and an eight-point that was two-and-a-half years old and was the one Jim was sure he had missed last year when he was much smaller, but still an eight-point.

The fourth buck in this group was the one that had his father and him talking for hours. He would be five-and-a-half years old by now and just about impossible to get close to. Rarely did he show himself in the daytime, and during hunting season, he seemed to cease to exist.

Jim had one close call with him last season and had learned a valuable lesson from it.

He had found a heavily used trail with some fresh scrapes along it as it came out of the cattails and through the hardwoods toward the field. Jim had hung his tree stand in an old maple downwind from the trail. That same afternoon he had climbed up in the stand and waited. Just before dark, an eight-point came walking down the trail moving towards the large scrape underneath his tree.

Just as Jim had started to draw his bow, he caught a movement out of the corner of his eye. He turned his head slowly and found his eyes on the largest set of horns he had ever seen. They were attached to the largest deer he had ever seen. He was only forty yards away and moving along the trail towards Jim.

The smaller buck had finished working the scrape and had moved further along the trail. Jim was shaking so badly he was certain the huge buck would spot him. The buck closed to thirty yards, then twenty-five, twenty. Another ten yards and he would be broadside. He was breathtaking. His rack was high and heavy with thick long points. He was totally attuned to everything going on around him and it was this alertness that saved him.

Just before he was within range, the smaller buck reached the point in the trail where Jim had crossed getting to his stand. The young buck became stiff-legged and his hair along his back bristled. The old buck instantly froze, his eyes on the younger buck. Both deer began raising their noses high in the air, trying to scent any danger in the area. Finally, with the air thermals moving downhill in the evening and moved around by the slight breeze, the younger buck eventually caught Jim's scent. In a flash, both bucks disappeared back into the cattails. It was then that Jim took to wearing rubber boots as he did for fox trapping.

There were only a few minutes of light left and Jim was beginning to believe that the group of bucks wasn't going to show up tonight. Just then, one of the six-pointers trotted out into the clover. He was closely followed by the other six-point. Jim glassed the two smaller bucks and was sure they were the same ones he'd been watching all summer.

He was proven correct when the eight-point suddenly appeared at the edge of the field. He seemed much larger than Jim had remembered, and for a second he thought maybe this was the big one. Then in the background behind the buck, as Jim was watching through the binoculars, he saw a set of huge antlers moving above the cattails. The deer itself could not be seen, just the antlers plainly visible, moving slowly towards the edge of the cover.

Jim felt his breath grow short and heard himself gasp as the buck's head finally appeared. Still the buck was in no hurry and stood cautiously checking for danger. Jim couldn't believe that he was actually bigger than last year. He was well over twenty inches across between his main beams, and his rack set almost two feet above his head. When he turned sideways, Jim could see that his main beams ran out past the end of his nose at least two or three inches.

The other deer were all busy feeding except for him. Jim's eyes were trained on him and only him. Still, he wouldn't step fully out of the cattails and Jim was left with this picture in his mind as the light finally gave way to darkness.

As Jim turned and slipped up the cornrow towards the

house, careful not to spook the deer still feeding in the darkness, he felt an excitement and anticipation for the hunting season he had never felt before. With a little luck and some planning and hard work, maybe, just maybe, he would get his chance at the monster.

Across the clover up in the hardwoods on another knoll, a different man was also planning the big buck's demise. He was neither awed nor inspired by the beauty of the animal. He saw him simply in terms of dollars and cents. The meat sold on the black market and the horns to the highest bidder. He figured at least a thousand dollars if not more for a rack that size.

A plan was forming already, not here or now, but when the time and place came together. He would wait until the buck showed himself on the other side of Black Creek and Jackson's Swamp. Old man Jackson had a hayfield on the west side of his swamp and the big buck's track showed he frequented it regularly.

There would be no bow, no license. His rifle and spotlight had brought down many deer in the past and this one would be no different, maybe just take a little longer.

Feeling sure of his plan, Jubal Hayes turned and disappeared into the night.

Matt Buche

.

Chapter 4

  Not being old enough to drive had presented Jim with the problem of how to get back and forth from work each Saturday. After much deliberation Jim and his mom had decided to try having Jim ride his bike the five miles into town, then Ann would come up just before closing with the truck to pick up the week's supply of feed and give Jim a ride home.
  A good solution as long as it didn't rain, Jim thought, as he turned his bike into the highway for the last mile and a half into town. He didn't mind the ride. It was all through the woods except for this last part. He had even left a little early this morning so he could check under the bridge over Black Creek for any mink tracks.
  Two sets of tracks showed in the wet sand along the cement wall. One set was much smaller, probably a female, the other, a much larger set, that had to belong to the same big buck mink

that had eluded Jim's traps last year.

There were also muskrat and coon tracks visible along the two trails that ran underneath the road. Plenty of fur sign, as usual. Jim had already planned where he would place each trap come opening day.

Jim pulled into the parking lot of the elevator and leaned his bike up against the cement steps leading into the office.

Stan Porter opened the office door and called out, "Mornin', Jim, see you made it. You can head out to the loading dock and see Ortin, he'll show you around."

Ortin Taylor had worked at the feed mill for as long as Jim could remember. This was part of the reason Jim was excited about working here. Ortin was famous in the area as an expert fox trapper. Several years back he had taken over one hundred fox in a single season. This was not counting all the muskrats, coon, and mink he took that year as well.

When November rolled around, the elevator needed to stay open nearly twenty-four hours a day to handle all the incoming corn and to keep the corn dryers running continuously. This allowed Ortin to work nights, and then run his traps first thing in the morning. He would catch a few hours sleep in the afternoon, then skin in the evening before heading in for his shift.

Jim spotted Ortin standing next to some fifty-pound bags of horse feed neatly stacked four per level on a wooden pallet at the end of the loading dock. He was a tall man, over six feet, but slim with broad shoulders and hands that looked almost too large for the rest of his body. He was wearing a weathered red cap that advertised the brand of seed corn sold at the elevator. His black hair showed traces of gray as it peeked out from the sides of his cap. His hair was cut short, a reminder of his days in the military, which he spoke of only rarely.

Jim climbed the steps up to the loading dock feeling quite self-conscious; as he knew Ortin had been watching him all the way across the parking lot.

"Well, I see my new help has arrived," Ortin said, "and

early too. How ya doin', Jim?"

"Fine, Mr. Taylor. Mr. Porter said that you'd tell me what needed to be done."

"Not much to it, Jim. You'll help me bag feed when someone wants a custom-made order, or if someone needs a bag of horse feed or rabbit pellets loaded in their car, that's your job. Mostly it's what we have out here that you'll be handling, but if someone needs a block of salt or whatever from the office, they'll buzz you to come up. If we get slow, we may do a little cleaning or maybe just chew the fat." Ortin was smiling.

"The times I've been up here with Dad getting feed on Saturdays, it sure has seemed busy." Jim nudged the pile of bags with the toe of his shoe.

"Saturday mornings are when all the hobby farmers come to get their feed," Ortin said. "You know, like the people who have a couple of horses or some rabbits. They don't make their main living off their livestock. They work somewhere and just have a few animals on the side."

Jim looked up. "I guess we'd be considered hobby farmers too, since Dad works construction and just farms on the side."

"No," Ortin said, "you've got farming in your backgrounds, in your blood. Your grandpa farmed that ground all his life." He pushed his cap back and scratched his chin. "Sure do miss your grandpa," Ortin said, looking out across the parking lot. A dusty gray Ford pickup turned into the elevator. "They don't make 'em like him anymore."

The truck stopped at the office. "That's Burton Marlow, he'll be wanting a batch of hog feed mixed up for that bunch of new feeder pigs he just bought." Two more vehicles pulled into the parking lot. "Well, Jim, looks like we're going to be busy after all. Don't be afraid to ask questions either. Everybody here will help you out at first. Just be nice to the customers and try not to keep 'em waiting and everything will go just fine."

Jim nodded and started to speak just as the buzzer from the office sounded from across the lot. Jim jumped off the loading dock and trotted towards the office not feeling quite as nervous as before.

The morning passed quickly and by noon, Jim knew where most everything was stored. As Ortin had said, Jim's job consisted mostly of loading a bag or two of rabbit pellets, chicken starter, or horse feed in the back of the customers' cars. Most of the people Jim knew or went to school with their children.

The elevator on Saturday mornings was almost like a social gathering place. Many times the office became quite crowded as the customers backed up because some conversation about the weather, crops, or politics had become quite involved. Then one of the participants would realize they had some other errands yet to run and hurried off, usually while still trying to make some point as they made their way out the door.

Jim's uneasiness had all but been erased by the time he saw his mother pull into the parking lot.

"You want the same batch of feed you had mixed up last weekend, Jim?" Ortin asked.

"Yeah, and I'll need some extra starter pellets too," Jim said.

Ortin wheeled the feed cart first to the soybean meal bin and measured out the precise weight needed and dumped it into the elevator leg to be carried up to the overhead mixer. He then filled the cart full with ground corn meal and dumped it into the mixer. He added a couple of hand scoops of minerals and the batch was completed.

Ann came out of the office and backed the pickup up to the dock. Jim jumped into the back, grabbed the stack of bags, and threw them up next to the mixer. Ann stepped out of the truck and stood by the cab, shielding her eyes from the sun with one hand.

"Well, Ortin," she said, "have you been keeping Jim busy this morning?"

Ortin smiled. "I haven't had to, Ann. That buzzer from the office has been doing it for me."

Ortin slipped each bag over the spout that angled out from the bottom of the mixer and pulled the slide out which allowed the feed to fall into the bag. When the bag was full, he replaced the slide, swung the full bag over to Jim to tie, and then repeated the process. Jim tied the bags, and then loaded them into the back of the truck.

He watched Ortin's muscles flex as he swung each bag over to him and marveled at what great shape he kept himself in. Most men his age had accumulated a layer of fat around the waist. Not Ortin. Certainly working at the elevator helped, but Jim knew that being an outdoorsman played a major part. Jim hoped he would be the same way when he was older.

When the last bag was tied and thrown in the truck, Jim went inside to grab two bags of starter pellets.

Ortin turned to Ann. "If there is anything you and Jim need while Ray's away, you just let me know."

Ann smiled and nodded. "Thanks. I think we'll be all right though. Things have gone pretty smoothly so far."

Jim returned with the two bags and threw them on top of the other feed. Then he helped Ortin turn off all the lights and shut all the doors as it was now 1:00 p.m.

"Jim, I'll write your hours down this week, but next week we'll have you start punching the time clock," Ortin said. "You'll also get your first paycheck next week."

"Good," Jim said, as he laid his bike in the back of the truck. "I've only got three hunting arrows left and bow season opens in a couple of weeks."

Ortin leaned his lanky frame against the loading dock door and pushed his cap back so the bill was sticking straight up. "Well, if you need help tracking one or dragging one out, just give a holler."

"Thanks. I'll see ya' next Saturday." He climbed into the cab and waved.

When they had pulled onto the road, Ann said, "You must have made a good impression on Ortin today. He was offering help left and right."

Jim nodded. "I think he thought a lot of Grandpa."

"A lot of people did," Ann said.

As Ortin started down the steps of the loading dock to head to his truck, he stopped abruptly. A dirty black Chevy pickup came sputtering across the railroad tracks and passed by the office. Ortin recognized the driver, and a small knot formed in the furrow across his brow. He wondered if Jubal Hayes knew that Ray Parker was out of town and that Ann and the boy were all alone.

He knew the answer already. "Same way a coyote finds a kill by hearing the magpies bickering," Ortin said aloud. "And no one knows better than me that Jubal Hayes is one clever coyote."

He tugged his cap back down across his forehead and turned towards his truck parked at the far end of the lot.

Chapter 5

Jim nestled his shoulder against the trunk of the huge oak and took a deep breath. Opening day had finally arrived. He hadn't hunted this morning because it was a school day, but as soon as he had gotten home, he hurried through his chores, changed his clothes, and grabbed his bow.

There hadn't been time before season to find a place to hang his portable stand, so he headed for the old oak that grew along the edge of the willows right where the corn ended and the clover began.

His grandfather had helped him build the stand three years ago. It was no more than two boards nailed to two branches that paralleled each other as they left the trunk approximately fifteen feet above the ground.

Really all his grandfather had done was to hand the boards up to Jim so he could nail them in place. Then Jim had stepped out as far as he could and cut the branches off so he would have a window to shoot through.

His grandfather wouldn't allow any nails to be placed in the trunk. He loved that tree too much. So there were no steps, but none was really needed, as one branch was only about eight feet off the ground. Jim simply jumped up, grabbed the limb, and pulled himself up. Once up in the tree it was easy climbing from there. When he reached the platform, he slipped on his safety harness and pulled his bow up with a string that he had tied around a branch and hung down to the ground.

The stand couldn't have been in a better location either. It was quick and easy to get to and allowed Jim to hunt it when the wind was blowing from several directions. Only if the wind was directly out of the north or east did he avoid using the stand. The tree was the only one of any size along the edge of the swamp. It was mostly all young willows with a few elms here and there.

Being a white oak only made it better. When the huge tree dropped its acorns in early October, it was like a dinner bell sounding for the deer.

With the onset of the rut, its low-hanging branches were favored by the bucks for making scrapes. In fact, there was one scrape that stayed open all year. Whenever the deer passed by they would stop and lick, smell, and rub their faces on the one branch in particular. Jim had read about these licking branches. It was more or less a way deer kept track of each other through the year. Just a way to say, "I was here."

Jim relaxed. It was hard to believe his father had been gone a month already. They had received several letters and he had called every Sunday evening. Everything was going fine and he expected to be back shortly before Christmas.

Jim had filled him in about the livestock. He had gotten the first litters weaned and all into one pen and put the sows out with the market hogs. The second batch of sows had already had their litters. They had all had them over a three-day period. Jim was relieved it was over and that there hadn't been any major problems.

The six sows had a total of seventy-five little ones and only seven had died. Jim and Ann had kept a close eye on them. They hadn't gotten much sleep the first couple of nights and Ann would run home during her lunch break each day to check on them.

The litters were all a week old now and had been given their iron shots. Barring an outbreak of scours or a sow lying or stepping on one, there wasn't too much danger of losing many more.

The sudden scolding he received from a large fox squirrel high above him broke Jim's thoughts. Concluding that Jim was no danger to him, he continued to gather acorns, occasionally dropping one that bounced its way down from branch to branch to the ground.

This had been Jim's first real chance to relax since his father had left. Still, he felt good about how everything had been going.

He looked forward to working each Saturday morning with Ortin, as most of the day they talked about hunting and trapping while they worked. Ortin had given him some trapping tips and Jim was anxious for season to start so he could try them out.

Jim was amazed not only by Ortin's knowledge of wildlife, but also by how he used that knowledge. He had learned that Ortin was not only an expert fox trapper, but an avid bow hunter and fisherman as well. He could identify every tree, most plants, and birds as well.

Jim had also learned that Ortin was a widower and that it had been over fifteen years since his wife had passed away. Ortin had never remarried and seemed content to remain single.

An acorn bounced past Jim's head. There was less than an hour left before dark. Jim began to think the only things he would see would be the squirrel and the mosquitoes, which had just announced their arrival by buzzing inside his ear. The breeze earlier had kept them at bay, but now that the wind had died down, he realized he would be at their mercy.

He kept watch toward the corner of the field where the cattails, willows, clover and hardwoods all came together. At the end of the ridge of hardwoods that tapered down to meet the willows and cattails was where Jim expected to see the deer emerge. The same spot where he had seen the big buck a month earlier. Occasionally he would glance back to the south end of the clover and along the west end of the corn, which was right in line with the oak.

He was down to less than ten minutes of shooting light left when he glanced once more to his left along the corn and was startled by the sight of a six-point walking directly towards the oak tree. The buck was only thirty yards away and moving steadily closer.

There was no time to get nervous. Jim simply stood straight, moving his shoulders away from the tree. His feet were already in position should the buck walk into his shooting lane. He'd already nocked his arrow. He tightened his grip on the bow and waited.

The buck came to the edge of the tree's outlying branches and stopped. If the buck turned to his left, he would walk directly where Jim wanted him.

The breeze had died completely by now and the only sound came from the growing horde of mosquitoes that were biting him nonstop.

It took everything he had to keep from swatting them. It was precisely for this reason, that Jim usually enjoyed hunting more after a couple of good frosts.

But then again, he thought, you couldn't shoot one from the sofa either. He wouldn't be this close right now if he worried about being bit a few times.

Just as he thought he could stand it no longer, the buck turned and started walking into his shooting lane.

The buck's antlers were white, bleached by the sun. His coat was reddish brown with the white patch on his throat well defined and his nose black and wet.

He was a beautiful animal, a fat and healthy year-and-a-half old buck.

Jim tried to soak in everything about him. He could even see the long whiskers around his nose and mouth.

The buck had started into the opening and looked as if he had decided on where he wanted to go. When he reached the overhanging branch in the center of Jim's shooting lane he stopped. This was the moment Jim had been waiting for.

It was all done in one motion. The buck was broadside and only twelve yards away when he picked a tuft of hair, drew, anchored, and released just as the buck started forward with his right front leg.

The arrow sank deep in the buck's chest, stopping just short of the white fletching.

The buck kicked his back feet straight in the air and was instantly at full speed headed across the clover towards the hardwoods.

Jim watched him disappear into the woods, making a mental note of exactly where he entered.

He looked down at his bow, then back at the woods. Had this really happened or was he daydreaming again? He looked once again at his bow and the quiver containing only three arrows. He felt his legs begin to shake and his breath came in short, rapid gasps.

It had all happened so quickly. He leaned back up against the tree for a moment before climbing down. He felt good about the shot, and even though it was slightly high, he was certain he had gotten both lungs.

As he lowered his bow to the ground, he thought about how everything had been going his way lately. No problems with the livestock. Classes were going fine. His loved his new job at the elevator, and now a good hit on a nice buck on opening day.

He untied the bow and stepped out into the clover. There were only a few hairs where the buck had been when he shot. No problem. He would check where he entered the woods to pick up the blood trail.

First, he would let the buck go for a good hour. He would

head back to the house, eat something, grab the lantern and his knife, and start tracking him then.

As he turned towards the corn, he took a deep breath, feeling more alive at this moment than he could ever remember. "Yes," he said aloud as he disappeared into the corn, "this is going to be a great fall."

Chapter 6

Jim burst through the back door into the kitchen.

"Don't tell me you got that big buck the first night out?" Ann said. She was slowly stirring a pot simmering on the stove.

"No, but I got a good shot in on a nice six-point," Jim said as he peeled off his camo jacket. "It was right behind the shoulder, should be through both lungs. But I'm still going to let him go for a couple of hours."

"Good, because supper will be ready in a few minutes," Ann said. She began setting the table.

Jim washed up, then came back in the kitchen and finished setting the table.

"Do you think you'll need any help? I could call Ortin. He said he would give you a hand dragging one out."

"No, I should be able to drive the tractor back to the edge of the woods. I don't think he'll be too far from there." Jim pulled out his hunting knife and sat down at the table. Running his finger along the blade to check the sharpness, he continued, "I just hope he ends up on this side of Black Creek. Otherwise, I'll have to drive around to Jackson's side of the swamp. I guess I should wait 'till I find him before I figure out how to get him out though," Jim said, flashing a smile.

Ann spooned a hefty pile of pork and beans onto Jim's plate. The huge chunks of ham looked more like steaks than the bits of meat usually found in canned beans. These were homemade the beans from the Johnson's down the road, and the ham from their own hogs. A fresh loaf of bread, hot and steaming from the oven with real butter, was a full meal in itself. The two together were enough to stick to the ribs of any man.

Jim wiped his plate clean with his last bit of bread and popped it in his mouth. Ann spoke without looking up from her plate. "There's no reason to eat like a hog just because we raise them." A slight smile formed as she spoke.

"Sorry, Mom, but you're always telling me to clean my plate." He got up, took his plate to the sink, and rinsed it off. He looked out the window, checked the clock, and said, "By the time I get the lantern, fire up the tractor, and get back there, it will be almost two hours since I shot him."

"Do you want me to go back with you," Ann said, starting to clean the table.

"No thanks, Mom, I'll be fine. If I have any trouble, I'll just gut him and leave him 'til morning. It's suppose to get down to forty degrees tonight."

"I'll wait up just the same. You be careful around that creek. Your grandpa always said that was the thickest stretch of creek in Michigan."

Jim smiled as he put his coat back on. "Yeah, it's nasty down there all right, but that's why it's such good hunting." Jim headed toward the door to the garage. "Be back in a couple of hours."

On the wall in the garage, next to where Jim kept his bow, hung an old Coleman lantern. Jim took the lantern off the nail and shook it. He heard the fuel slosh back and forth in the tank. He took a quick look to see that both mantles were intact and Jim headed out the door towards the barn.

The John Deere 30/20 was the workhorse around the farm. They plowed, planted, cut hay, hauled manure whatever needed to be done the 60-horse tractor did it all.

Jim jumped up on the tractor, turned the key, and pushed the starter button. A slow groan sounded as the engine tried to turn over, then nothing but the clicking of the starter. Jim knew it was no use; the battery was dead.

Jim thought of driving the truck back down the lane but that would still leave a long drag. The jumper cables wouldn't reach because Jim had driven the tractor straight in instead of backing it in. The manure spreader was still hooked on so there was no way to get close.

Jim decided to hook up the battery charger to the tractor and leave it charging over night. He would head back to find the deer, field dress him, and then go back in the morning to haul him out.

Straight west of the house where the corn met the yard was a wide gap between two rows of corn. This gap ran the entire length of the field and ended at the middle of the clover field.

Jim walked this gap all the way and then cut across the hayfield to the spot where he had last seen the buck. He felt sure the buck had entered where a well-worn trail came out of the creek bottom, ran up over the ridge, and came out to the edge of the clover.

Holding the lantern low and moving it slowly from side to side, Jim searched the trail where it broke from the woods. He scanned the grass and what few leaves were on the ground. Finally, after he had searched into the woods ten feet or so, he spotted a large patch of blood along the left side of the trail. Sweeping the lantern off to the side, he spotted many smaller drops in a sprayed pattern on the small bushes that the trail cut through.

Moving slowly and only going forward after finding more blood, Jim worked his way up the trail towards the top of the ridge. At the top, the trail turned southwest and down the other side of the ridge.

The trail of blood was almost continuous now, but still only on the left side of the trail. Jim was both relieved and concerned. The arrow had gone through, but if he had hit both lungs squarely, there would be blood on both sides of the trail. Still the blood was becoming more and more plentiful as Jim moved at a quicker pace.

The trail entered the thicker brush along the creek bottom. Jim was certain the buck must be just ahead. However, another thirty yards ahead was Black Creek and the trail was cutting through a tangle of willows mixed with patches of multi-flower rose. Jim hunched over as far as he could without crawling.

The trail turned west and paralleled the creek. The ground was soft and Jim's boots were beginning to sink in a few inches. The buck's tracks were mixed in with a myriad of other tracks going in both directions. Fighting the brush with one hand while trying to keep the lantern from being tangled, and all the while fighting to keep his balance, was beginning to wear on him.

Suddenly Jim stopped and knelt closer to ground. No blood. Swinging the lantern out in front of him farther showed only the black muck churned up by the countless deer tracks.

Jim backtracked until he found the last blood visible on the trail. He searched the north side of the trail thinking the buck might have weakened and was attempting to circle around to watch his back trail before bedding down. Working his way out about ten yards from the trail, and then circling back in both directions towards the trail, he found no blood.

Starting back at the last blood, he swung the lantern out above the south side of the trail towards the creek. There, five yards out from the trail, was a large pool of blood. Apparently, the buck had jumped off the trail to this spot and then stood there for a moment before crossing the creek.

Jim walked past the blood to the edge of the creek. The swirling black water looked more like a river in the light cast from the lantern.

Jim hadn't thought of having to cross the creek. There was no way the buck should have come this far. By his estimate, the deer had now traveled all of two hundred yards from where Jim had shot him.

    Searching along the creek back to the east, Jim finally found what he was looking for. The old ash tree had died the summer before last. After its roots dried out and the spring rains had raised the levels of the creek, the dead tree had been leaning. Late last spring during a strong thunderstorm, the old tree had finally come crashing down across the creek.

    Jim slowly worked his way onto the log. Holding the lantern in his outstretched hand out over the log, he sidestepped his way along. Half way across, he looked down into the water rushing by. The creek made a sharp turn just after it passed under the log, and a large pool formed against the backside where the water cut underneath the bank. Small whirlpools formed and then disappeared as water realigned itself and moved on downstream.

    It wasn't particularly deep here. Jim had fished this hole before, that's how he knew about the tree. Still the last thing he wanted was to end up going for a dip.

    Reaching the other side, Jim worked back up the creek until he recognized the spot on the opposite side where he found the last blood.

    Jim stepped around a tangle of briars next to the creek that blocked his way and nearly stepped on the buck.

    Jim jumped back. He swung the lantern carefully out in front of him. Realizing that the buck was dead, he sat down to catch his breath.

    There was darkness all around except for the glow from the lantern. The only sounds were the creek winding its way through the brush and the hiss from the lantern.

    Jim ran his hands over the buck's white horns, touching each point. He felt the smoothness of his coat as he stroked the hair along his neck.

    It was with respect and admiration that Jim gazed upon his buck. His buck, he thought. He had taken this deer's life and now it was his responsibility to use as much of it as possible.

Taking his tag out of his coat pocket, he cut out the date and number of points on each antler and fastened the tag to the buck's antler.

As Jim reached down to begin field dressing the buck, the lantern sputtered and suddenly dimmed. "Crap," he said aloud. He would have to hurry. He only had a minute or so before the old lantern would give out.

Quickly Jim spread the deer's hind legs and made an incision starting near the rectum and running straight up to the sternum, careful not to go any deeper than just through the skin so he would not puncture the intestines or stomach. Just as he finished making the cut, the lantern gave one last gasp and went out.

Standing in the dark, Jim waited a few moments for his eyes to adjust. Soon he could see the outline of the deer, and then gradually a little more of the surroundings became visible. Finally, when he could safely continue, Jim felt his way through the rest of the job. Reaching as far up into the chest cavity as he could, he cut the windpipe and pulled out the heart and lungs. Then he cut away the diaphragm and pulled out the rest of the entrails. Reaching down into the pelvic area, Jim felt for the bladder and ran his hand around it until he located the urethra and pinched it off with his fingers. He cut through it above his fingers and pulled the bladder free.

That would have to do for now he thought. The deer would keep overnight. He would bring the tractor around tomorrow morning, drive down the lane in Jackson's hayfield, and should have only a hundred yards or so to drag the deer.

Not wanting to try and find his way back through the woods with no light, Jim decided to cut straight west through the brush. When he came out into Jackson's hayfield, he would head south, hit the road, and head home. It would take a while longer but it was better than busting brush in the dark.

Jim worked his way through the brush and finally emerged into the rolling hayfield. Angling southwest, Jim found the lane and started toward the road.

The lane ran straight east for a distance, topped a small rise, and started angling southeast. It wasn't a lane as much as just a two track, no fencerows on either side, just the worn tracks free of any growth. The walking was easy and Jim felt good in the cool night air.

As Jim topped the rise, the field was suddenly awash in light. It took a moment before he realized exactly what was happening. He recognized the piercing ray as a spotlight.

Jim knew there must be a vehicle, but the glare from the light kept him from picking up its outline.

Looking back into the field to his right, Jim was startled to see a six-point buck standing scarcely seventy-five yards away staring directly into the beam. The deer could have been the twin to the buck he had just shot.

Jim hadn't finished the thought when the crack of the rifle sounded. The buck dropped like a rock and rolled onto his side with his legs stiff and straight. A moment later, he went limp and lay still.

Stunned, Jim stared at the motionless deer. Suddenly the light swung over Jim and then down to the ground and then against the truck itself. Instantly Jim recognized the vehicle and a cold chill moved up his neck and across his scalp.

The spotlight had no more than swung across the truck when it shot back to Jim.

For an instant Jim was frozen. However, the thought of the deer in the same position only a few seconds before sent a wave of fear through Jim and instinct took over. He ran.

Down the hill toward the willows, which looked like huge blades of grass as they stood against the far edge of the light from the spotlight, Jim was running as fast as he could with his boots catching in the tangle of hay shoots. He felt his heart pumping madly and strangely; he wondered, whether it was beating from the running or the fear he felt.

He watched the willows grow closer and wondered why no shot came. With fifty yards left to the willows, he heard the truck engine start. The spotlight, which still held Jim in its beam, wavered and then went out.

Jim hit the wall of willows in total blackness as his eyes were once again fighting to adjust to the moonless night.

The sound of the truck's engine accelerating and growing nearer spurred Jim through the tangle of underbrush. He felt the sting of briars as they ripped across his face, penetrated his jeans, and raked his thighs.

Suddenly he was in mid-air and realized what had happened just before he hit the water. His legs churned in the water and pushed him towards the far side of the creek.

Jim crawled up on the bank just as he heard the truck stop next to the willows. He lay still and tried to quiet his breathing. He heard the truck door squeak as it opened.

"Hey boy," Jim cringed at the sound of the voice. "You're that Parker boy, I know you." Jim pulled his legs to his chest.

"You keep your mouth shut 'bout what you saw tonight, boy. I know your daddy ain't home to protect you and your momma. You give me trouble, boy, and I'll shore 'nuff give you more than just trouble back. You hear me, boy? Keep your mouth shut." The anger in the words drove into Jim's body like the growing cold.

Jim heard the truck start and pull away with the headlights off. He heard it stop again, then the sound of the tailgate being opened, and a few seconds later close again, then the sound of the truck moving again and finally moving off growing more faint.

Jim lay there in the dark for some time with only the sound of the creek rushing by behind him. Slowly he sat up. Touching his cheek, Jim felt a warm sticky trail running off his face and down his neck. He pulled his boots off and dumped the water back into the swirling creek below him.

Jim slipped his boots back on and stood up. He looked above the brush and through the hardwoods above Black Creek and saw the faint glow of the light in the old farmhouse. Pulling his collar up and taking one last look back across the creek towards the hayfield, Jim headed towards home with the words of Jubal Hayes still ringing in his ears.

Chapter 7

Jim slid his fingers along the string to the arrow. The huge buck was walking straight towards him. Just a few more steps and he would be broadside and only ten yards away.

The buck's long tines glistened in the sunlight. His neck was swollen and his muscles rippled as he walked by Jim's stand.

Jim slowly started his draw, his eyes trained on the buck's vitals.

The crack of the rifle and the buck dropping were all one.

Jim froze as the brush parted and Jubal Hayes stepped forward.

Shrinking back against the tree trunk, Jim's heart pounded madly. He tried not to look but couldn't stop himself. The hideous grin on Hayes' face chilled him to the bone as he looked Jim straight in the eye.

Jim's feet felt nailed to the tree as Jubal Hayes slowly raised his rifle, laughing, his yellow teeth glowing. He couldn't move. There was no escape. He closed his eyes, and waited for the shot to come, his fingers digging into the bark of the tree.

No shot came and Jim slowly opened his eyes and found himself in the middle of a hay field staring directly into the beam of a spotlight. The same evil laugh sounded from the source of the light.

Jim tried to run, but his feet seemed weighted down. The brush line was just ahead, but he could not get any closer. The tangle of alfalfa grabbed at his boots, slowing him down even more. All the while, he could hear the sound of a truck racing towards him, growing louder and accelerating. There was no escape.

Jim sat straight up in bed as reality rushed into his head. He put his hand on his chest and felt his heart pounding wildly. Slowly the dream faded away and Jim collapsed back onto his bed and pulled the covers over his head.

When his heart slowed down, Jim pulled off the covers and peered out his window, as the first weak light of dawn showed through.

The events of the night before played through his head. He wished it all had been a dream, but there was no changing the fact; it had all happened.

The worst part was that he had lied to his mother. He hadn't really lied; he just left out a whole lot. He told her the lantern went out and that he cut himself while busting through the brush with no light. But that was it. No deer shot in the hayfield, no being chased, no threats, nothing.

He couldn't help but wonder what his dad or grandpa would have done. No one would doubt their word. It would have been no problem at all just call the conservation officer or State Police and that would be that.

This was different. He was fifteen, a kid. He hadn't actually seen Jubal Hayes even though he was sure it was his truck and his voice. He was also certain there was no evidence of the deer being shot. By the sound of his truck, he had just thrown the deer in the back and left.

Maybe there were tracks left by the truck. Empty cartridges left on the ground; blood, hair, anything.

Jim got up and began dressing. Who was he kidding? There was no way Hayes took that deer to his house. For all Jubal knew, Jim had gone straight home and called the police.

Jim looked back out the window just as a large flock of geese was landing on the lake.

He glanced around his room. An old poster advertising Hawbaker's trapping lure hung on the wall next to his gun rack. His dresser, next to his bed, was covered with back issues of Fur-Fish-Game. A picture of his grandfather and his dad with a stringer of trout from their last fishing trip up on the Au Sable River hung over the dresser.

His desk was in front of the window that looked south towards the creek and Jackson's hayfield.

He could see the hayfield barely, through the trees. It looked much different in the morning light.

He dressed and went down the stairs. A pan of cut potatoes was frying right next to the pan of bacon, but Jim sat down at the table and stared out the window towards the barn.

Ann poked at the frying bacon, "Awfully quiet for being such a great hunter."

"Just tired, Mom," Jim rubbed his eyes and stretched.

"Are you going to take the truck around and get your deer or see if the tractor starts?"

I'll just take the truck if it's all right with you. It will be a lot quicker," Jim said.

Ann brought two plates over, one piled high. "That's fine. It's only a half mile down to Jackson's Lane." Ann sat down across the table from Jim. "Hope you're hungry. Sometimes I forget I'm just cooking for the two of us."

Jim wished his dad were here now. He wouldn't have lied to his mom. As much as he hated lying to her, he didn't want to worry her with this. She had enough on her mind. Besides, if he kept his mouth shut, there wouldn't be any problem. Still, something about that didn't set right either.

He was tired of thinking about it.

The steaming plate in front of him reminded him how hungry he was. He dug in.

Ann poured herself a cup of coffee. "I thought you'd be hungry this morning, as whipped as you looked last night."

Jim finished his plate and drank down a glass of milk. "Well, I'd better hurry up and do chores before I go get him. I'll still end up being late for school" Jim headed towards the door.

"I'll call the store and tell them I'll be a few minutes late too," Ann hollered as Jim went outside.

Not very excited about getting a buck on opening day, Ann thought, as she started dishes.

Jim hurried through his chores, all the while wondering what he should do. He couldn't get the thought of his grandfather and the contempt he had for poachers out of his head. He felt ashamed for being afraid, but that didn't change the fact that he was.

Jim climbed into the pickup and started the engine. He didn't have his driver's license yet, but growing up on a farm, young boys learned to drive early. Besides, it was only a half mile down the road.

Jim steered the pickup down the long driveway and turned onto the road. The drive into Jackson's hayfield was not very well marked and Jim almost missed it. As he pulled into the field, he could see why Jubal chose this spot. You could pull a short way into the field and be completely hidden. The thick growth along the road obscured any view into the field. Then if you followed the lane for a short distance, it angled downhill and out of sight.

Jim kept an eye peeled for anything that might be considered evidence, but there were tracks all over. The hay had been cut a month or so back and had grown back since then. About eight or nine inches, Jim guessed. He couldn't get over the number of tracks crisscrossing the field. He wondered who else had been out here and how many other deer had been shot.

The lane wound down and finally paralleled the willows along the creek bottom. Jim parked the truck there in the lane. No matter that everyone else drove all over the field, he wasn't going to.

He knew about where he came out into the field last night and headed in that direction. He no more than stepped into the willows when he spotted one of his boot tracks. It was obviously made after he had left his buck, since it was headed out of the brush.

Working his way through the undergrowth, he was soon standing over his deer. It had been cool enough last night so there was no chance of him spoiling, but he certainly couldn't leave him here all day.

Jim knelt down and lifted the buck's head off the ground. It was going to be hard dragging this stiff deer through the brush. Too bad, he hadn't had a chance to feel good about having gotten a buck. He wondered somehow if that was also being disrespectful to the deer. An animal should be appreciated. It goes along with all the emotions that come with harvesting an animal. He wondered if Jubal Hayes appreciated deer the way he did. He knew the answer. No one who appreciated them would blast them while they stood staring into a spotlight.

Jim would stop and rest, admire the buck, than drag some more. He was right; it was tough going. The deer's legs kept hanging up on the willows. There really wasn't any trail here, so Jim just plowed on through the brush. He could see the field edge up ahead about thirty yards and the truck another thirty yards out in the field.

There was no sound except for his own breathing and the quiet only reminded Jim of how alone he was right now. He thought of how totally alone he had felt last night and it was the first time he could remember being scared out in the woods. He reached down, grabbed the buck's antlers, and started pulling. The sound of feet rushing through the leaves to his left spun Jim around with his fists clenched and his heart pounding.

The sight of the cottontail bounding harmlessly away both relieved and angered him. His face reddened even though no one was there to witness his short-lived panic attack. Angrily he grabbed the antlers and plowed forward.

Resting at the edge of the field, Jim looked out across the field and could see where he must have been standing when the deer was shot. He wondered whether Jubal knew about the huge buck Jim had been seeing. He hoped not, and the thought of the buck being shot under a spotlight turned Jim's stomach.

Jim reached the truck and dropped the tailgate. Holding the buck's head up with one hand, he crawled into the back of the truck, and with one big heave, pulled the deer into the back.

As he jumped into the cab and started the truck, Jim looked in the rear view mirror and caught his own reflection. *Admit it*, he thought, *you're scared and there's no other reason to keep you from telling. Like Grandpa used to say, you can hide from everybody else but you can't hide from yourself.* Jim drove the truck back up the lane towards home.

Chapter 8

Jim ran his hands across the heavy, black rubber of his new waders. "Feels just like Christmas morning except I bought my own present."

Ann smiled as she steered the truck around the chatter bumps in the road. "Well, I hope you like them. They only cost you nearly everything you've made the last month and a half."

"They'll pay for themselves when I take an extra thirty muskrats this year," Jim said, still not taking his eyes off the waders.

Ann maneuvered the truck down the road, speeding up where the road was smooth, and then slowing down when potholes appeared ahead. "I thought you'd be ready to go after that big buck again. It's been over two weeks since you shot that six- point. You haven't been out since. I didn't think you'd give up that easy."

Jim glanced quickly at his mother, and then relaxed as he saw the smile on her face, "Just thought I'd get as much of the work done around home as I could before the rut started. That way, I could spend as much time in the woods as possible when the hunting's the best."

The night in the hayfield seemed like yesterday. He had busied himself as much as possible since then, keeping the barns clean, fixing gates, mowing the lawn, raking leaves, on top of homework. It had been easy to find excuses not to go hunting.

As the truck passed the drive into Jackson's hayfield, Jim looked out across the rolling hills to the brush line along Black Creek. The thought of the huge buck bedded deep in the brush sent a wave of anticipation through Jim.

Ortin had asked him just today if he had been out hunting lately. In between customers, Jim had again told him about seeing the big buck late in August and his plans for ambushing him. "You aren't gonna get a shot at him from the barn," Ortin had said jokingly.

Ann slowed the truck once more as they crossed the bridge over the creek. Jim peered out the window into the dark water flowing through the dense mix of cattails and willows. "Guess maybe I'll go out tonight if it's all right with you, Mom."

Ann shifted the truck down a gear to start the climb up the hill on the other side of the creek. "Sure. I'll hold off on supper until you get back. Wouldn't your dad be surprised if you got that big buck?" She let off the gas as they crested the hill and started down the other side to their driveway.

A rooster pheasant strutted across the road in front of the truck then sped off into the underbrush as they drove past.

"Haven't seen many pheasants this year," Ann said, still dodging potholes. "There was that one flock we kept seeing by Jackson's hayfield all summer, but I haven't seen them lately."

Jim rolled down the truck window and stuck his head out, trying to spot the rooster in the mirror. "Yeah, between all the hawks, possum, and skunks after them, it's a wonder there's any left. Plus what they don't get, the foxes and long winters really put the hurt on."

Looking down along the edge of the road speeding by, he spotted several sets of deer tracks crossing the road going in both directions. Moving through here at night, he thought. He felt a sudden surge of energy.

"Back right up to the barn, Mom, and I'll unload the feed right now," Jim said, still hanging his head out the window.

Ann backed the truck around to the barn door and shut off the engine. "Well, I've got some laundry to do before supper."

Jim lowered the tailgate and began unloading the truck. He filled the feeder for the pigs he had just weaned first. Then he filled the feeder for the market hogs.

The pen for the sows that had their litters weaned did not have a feeder. The amount of feed they received each day was limited to keep them from gaining too much weight. An overweight sow tended to have smaller litters.

After Jim had stored the remaining feed in the barn, he took a bag out to the sows to dump in their trough.

A water line ran along the top of the fence that separated the pen of market hogs and sows. Near the middle of the fence, the water line dropped down and split into two different pens, one for each side. Jim checked each side to make sure they were working.

Carrying the bag on his shoulder, he leaned over and released his grip on the end of the bag, letting it spill out into the trough as he walked along, filling the entire length.

The sows crowded around, pushing Jim out of the way and fighting for position. The pecking order was soon reestablished, and the sows settled in to filling their bellies.

Jim looked around suddenly. Something was wrong, but he wasn't sure what. Turning back towards the feeding sows, he realized that something was missing. Quickly he counted the sows, eight. He counted again but came up the same. One was missing, Red.

Jim started walking the pen all the way around, looking

for where Red might have gotten out. There were no holes and all the gates were wired shut.

He jumped the fence into the pen with the market hogs, looking for her.

Red was the tamest sow they had. She would walk right up to you, hoping to get her daily scratching behind the ears. She was also the best mother. Hearing any squeals from her little ones, she would immediately jump up, so she rarely laid or stepped on one. You could also count on her throwing and raising at least a dozen little ones each time.

Finding no sign of her in with the market hogs, Jim jumped the fence and began circling the lot. As he rounded the corner at the far end near the loading chute, he stopped suddenly. A familiar knot began to form in the pit of his stomach.

It had rained two days ago, and the ruts leading up to the chute had filled in with water. The fresh mud and water on both sides of the rut indicated someone had backed up to the chute. By the looks of the mud slung all over the end of the chute, they had left in a hurry.

Jim followed the tracks out to where they joined the hardened driveway and disappeared except for the occasional clump of mud thrown from the treads.

Staring down the driveway towards the road, Jim suddenly felt lightheaded. He turned and started towards the house. There was no choice this time. He had to call the police. Even if he didn't mention Jubal's name, he could find a way to put them on the right trail.

He wasn't going to get away with this, not stealing from them. Jim felt his hands tighten into fists at the same time he realized he was running.

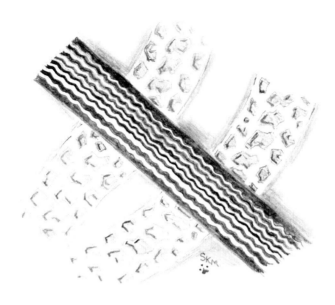

Chapter 9

Jim walked back and forth in the driveway; his hands buried in his pants pockets. Each time he turned back toward the house he could see his mother sitting on the front steps watching him.

"Jim," she finally said, "come over here, sit down. Pacing back and forth won't make Sheriff Raines get here any quicker."

Slowly he walked back to the house, his eyes fixed on the ground as if searching for answers in the dirt.

Ann stood up. "Why are you acting as if somehow this is your fault? You're much more upset about this than I am. Sure, I'm mad, but there really wasn't anything we could have done about it, was there?"

Jim looked up. "No, I guess not, but Dad won't be too happy about this."

A vehicle coming up the drive cut their conversation short.

Ann walked down the steps and past Jim. "We'll worry about that later."

Sheriff Raines stepped out of his car and smiled, "Ann, Jim, how you two doin'?" He spoke in a sure and calm tone. He had a way of making people feel at ease whenever he spoke. It was no wonder he was on his fifth term as county sheriff.

"Fine," Ann said, "other than we're minus one sow."

"Let's have a look at those tracks you mentioned on the phone," Sheriff Raines said as he started walking towards the barns.

Reaching the loading chute, Sheriff Raines bent over to inspect the tracks left by the thief. "There must be a hundred trucks in this area that have these tread works. I don't know if I could get the State Police to come out and do a casting of these tracks. They usually reserve that for more serious crimes."

Jim felt a wave of anger wash over him. He stepped past the sheriff and peered down at the two tire marks. "These look different from the other side. It must have two different brands of tires on the back."

The sheriff moved closer. "You're right, Jim. This track is from an off-road tire. You ever thought of going into police work, Jim?" the sheriff said and looking a little embarrassed. "I'll take a picture of the two tread marks and if I can get a lead on who was in the area at the time we might just make a case, Ann."

"I hope so, sheriff," Ann said. "Red was the best sow we had. She was also the tamest which made for easy pickings." The three walked back towards the sheriff's car.

"I do believe we are looking at one person working alone, though," Sheriff Raines said. "Why go to all the trouble to steal livestock and only take one animal unless you're all by yourself." He reached under the front seat and pulled out a Polaroid camera. "I know you folks don't get much traffic down here being it's a dead-end road and all, but if you've seen any pickups down here at all it might put us on the right track."

Ann and Jim looked at one another. "I haven't seen anyone other than the mail lady, how about you, Jim?" Ann said pulling her sweater closer as the evening wind grew colder. Jim's eyes swung towards the ground. "I saw an old black Chevy go by the other day. But I don't know who was driving." Jim nervously kicked a stone down the driveway, glancing from his mother to the sheriff and back to the ground.

"Jubal Hayes drives a black Chevy, and this whole situation smells just like him," Sheriff Raines said as he walked back towards the loading chute with the camera.

"Is there something else wrong, Jim? You seem a lot more upset than the situation calls for," Ann said. She stared intently at her son while he still kept his gaze on the ground.

"No." Jim sighed. "I just wanted things to go smoothly while Dad's gone. And now our best sow is gone."

Sheriff Raines walked back to his car. "I'll check out Jubal's truck and see if I can find anything. You should hear from me in a day or two. In the meantime, I'd chain and lock that gate to the loading chute. Let's not make it easy for whoever it was to do this again."

"Thanks, sheriff," Ann said. "I've got dinner on the stove, I'd better check on it." She turned and hurried across the yard towards the house.

Jim walked to the car window. "Sheriff, could you not mention the fact that I told you about seeing the black Chevy when you talk to Hayes?"

"Well, yes, I can for now, Jim, but if it goes to court it will come out. Any reason in particular you want to keep it quiet?" Sheriff Raines started his car.

"Well, I just feel like Mom and I have our hands full enough without worrying about Jubal Hayes being mad at us. Maybe it wasn't even him." Jim stepped back from the car as the sheriff slipped the car into gear.

"All right, Jim, I'll be discreet, but why don't you folks lock all your doors just the same?" Sheriff Raines waved as he backed out the driveway.

Jim watched as the sheriff drove away. Well, maybe he hadn't told the story exactly the way it happened, but he had seen Jubal Hayes down this road (even if it was in the middle of Jackson's hayfield).

Jim walked toward the barn as daylight began to fade. He stopped as a huge flock of Canadian geese came floating over the tree line north of the barn and began their descent onto the lake, which was glimmering in the evening light.

Chapter 10

Jim placed the bottle of lure back in the pack basket and stood back to admire his work.

The set was located on top of a ridge that ran for over a mile, intersected by a lane that ran for almost a half mile across the open field.

The hayfield had been cut three weeks ago for the last time this year, and had only grown back a couple of inches and probably wouldn't grow anymore now that there had been a couple of killing frosts.

The location had all the aspects needed for a hot spot to trap fox. Two long running travel lanes intersected each other in the middle of the hayfield that served as a food source. All this located in a section of great habitat. The only problem was that this was Jackson's hayfield and the memory of Jubal Hayes and that night a month ago still burned fresh in Jim's mind.

Giving the set one last look, Jim shouldered his backpack and turned towards the road. Jim had placed another identical set only eight feet away from this last set. Two sets placed close together but with different looks and lures used at each. One set had bait and lure to attract a fox if hungry. The other was set with a gland lure and a curiosity scent, which would interest a fox if it happened to have a full stomach and had no interest in the baited set.

Jim strode down the lane. He had set three locations today and still hoped to have time to bow hunt tonight. He hadn't been out in weeks, but with the leaves turning more each day, Jim's thoughts had returned to the huge buck that lived deep in the tangle of brush and cattails of Pratt Lake.

Ortin had come out the day after Red disappeared. He helped Jim boil and wax his fox traps. The two had spent the afternoon working on traps and discussing locations, and Ortin had shown Jim the proper way to construct a dirt hole set for fox.

Jim had learned more in that afternoon than he had in the past three years on his own and reading every article on fox sets in the pile of magazines stacked at the foot of his bed. Jim had realized several mistakes he had been making in the past and had been anxious all week to try out Ortin's advice. Jim had practiced making the set all week in the garden, giving special attention to bedding the trap properly so that it wouldn't tip if the animal were to step on the edge of the trap before stepping on the pan.

Ortin had encouraged him to set up three locations instead of just the hayfield at the back of their property. Aside from sets in their field, he would have two here in Jackson's, which was on the other side of Black Creek. Then a mile and a half to the south Jackson's had another hayfield that also bordered Black Creek.

"Great habitat in this area, not just here around the lake, but all along Black Creek," Ortin had said. "There are probably several litters of fox in this area. Then on top of that, later on when the litters break up in other areas, this creek is a travel lane for these young pups moving into new areas. So these spots could really produce a lot of fox if you keep your sets out for a full month."

They had talked at length also about Jim's chance of getting a shot at the huge buck. Once again, Ortin's advice had helped Jim realize he had been making some mistakes. "Don't hunt the same stand all the time. Have several placed and never hunt the same one twice in a row. This will keep bucks from patterning you, especially if you learn to sneak into your stands." Jim's head was spinning by the end of the day. Ortin knew more about wildlife than anyone he had ever met.

When Jim reached the road, he picked up his pace, though walking in the knee boots wasn't the most comfortable. They were necessary, though. The rubber kept any scent from being left at the set. He also wore them while bow hunting, but for nothing else. He never wore them in the barn, house or truck. He kept them clean of any odors.

Jim was walking into the wind as he headed towards home. He could feel that the temperature was falling and a line of blue-black clouds was pushing in from the northwest. Too cold to rain, Jim thought, but this front will have everything moving. He began to trot as he started up the hill on the other side of Black Creek. He would have just enough time to do chores and get back to the woods.

Matt Buche

Chapter 11

Jim leaned into the oak trying to blend in with the huge trunk. The doe and fawn had been feeding within twenty yards of him for the last ten minutes. Now they were moving directly downwind of him. Jim felt his muscles tense as he waited for the doe to wind him.

Five minutes later, the two deer still fed contentedly, downwind of Jim's perch eighteen feet in the air. Ortin was right, "Wear clean clothes and take a shower with scent free soap before you go out and you'll be amazed at how you can actually fool a deer nose for a few hours."

This stand was located another hundred yards deeper into cover from the stand he had seen the big buck from last year. On a small knoll between Black Creek and the west end of Pratt Lake, there were three white oaks. He placed his stand in the largest tree, which was in the center with the two smaller oaks on either side. The trees had dropped the majority of their acorns and the deer sign was everywhere.

Jim had hung the stand last Wednesday when he had the morning off because of a dental appointment. It had taken him only a half hour to put up the stand, as he didn't need to trim any branches from the tree or on the ground.

Jim hadn't been to this spot since last fall, but he knew that the deer fed heavily here when the acorns dropped. The two large scrapes on top of the knoll under the overhanging branches of the huge oak were more than enough to get Jim excited about sitting there.

The temperature continued to fall as the evening wore on. Jim slowly reached up and pulled his camouflage knit cap down over his ears as the two deer continued to feed among the scattered leaves below him.

It had been a hectic week, between the stolen hog last weekend, getting all his traps ready, putting up this stand, work at the feed mill earlier today, then getting all his traps set this afternoon. Still, he wouldn't have it any other way this time of year. There were only a few weeks to trap fox before the ground froze and the rut was the very best time to hunt the Pratt Lake Monster.

Every Saturday talk at the elevator had turned to the elusive buck. Fortunately, there were only three people who had permission to bow hunt in the area, and one of those was old man Jackson's nephew who lived out of town and only came to bow hunt for about three days before gun season opened. He rarely put up a tree stand, preferring to sneak around, mainly just looking for a good spot to sit on opening day of gun season.

The other was the Smith boy, Ron, who was two years older than Jim was and in his senior year at high school. His folks owned the farm on the other side of Pratt Lake, but Ron had a girlfriend and usually preferred talking about hunting to actually getting out there.

Of course, there was another person after the buck that cared nothing about having permission or seasons. Jim couldn't help but worry about what Jubal would try next. Strangely, though, Jim was no longer scared. He was angry. He had thought about it all week and decided that he would take no more.

Over the past two months, he had grown up a lot. Taking care of the farm by himself was only part of it. Working with Ortin and still making the honor roll at school had made Jim aware of what he was capable of with some hard work.

Jim had earned the respect of everyone at the elevator, most of all Ortin's. That was important to Jim and brought him to the realization that he had made a mistake by not turning Jubal in right away after that night in the hayfield. He was better than that and Jubal didn't deserve to be feared; only despised. That was what his grandfather would have said.

The sheriff had called earlier in the week, but had gotten nowhere. He had said that Jubal's truck had the same tires on the back and that he had no trailer around that the sheriff could find. He hadn't seemed very encouraging about getting Red back. Jim figured she was already cut, wrapped and frozen by now. The lock on the loading chute would make sure it wouldn't happen again, though.

The doe suddenly stiffened and stared intently toward the cover behind Jim. Jim tightened his grip on his bow but made no other move. His eyes stayed on the doe while he strained to hear any movement from behind. Several minutes passed with the doe alternately staring then feeding. The fawn was not interested and continued searching out the acorns hidden beneath the carpet of leaves.

Suddenly a low grunt broke the silence, quickly followed by another and then the sound of a deer walking. Jim listened intently and finally determined the deer would pass by his right side. This would mean he would have to turn almost 180 degrees in order to shoot. With the doe looking in his direction, Jim decided to wait.

The pounding in Jim's chest grew worse now that he could hear the deer moving towards him. He told himself he probably wouldn't get a shot, so just calm down. He had used this trick before when he felt the onset of buck fever.

Slowly Jim turned his head to the right, as the sound of the deer approaching grew louder. The doe continued to watch the approaching deer and failed to notice the movement of Jim's camouflage hat and face mask.

Suddenly the deer's head came into view and Jim felt himself draw a deep breath of the cool evening air. It was the same eight-pointer he had the close call with last year, only he was much bigger. The longest tines were nearly ten inches long.

As he glanced back toward the doe, Jim was surprised to see that another doe and two fawns had approached from the opposite direction. They, too, were staring in the buck's direction.

Jim was literally surrounded by deer, but the buck had his full attention. He was beautiful. Truly, a trophy and Jim had decided that given the chance, he would try to harvest this buck even though he knew the monster buck was still in the area.

As the minutes crawled along, the buck began feeding only ten yards away from where Jim pressed against the huge oak trunk. With the large number of acorns that had fallen in past days, the buck scarcely moved as he fed steadily. The does resumed feeding as the buck ignored them, more interested in filling his belly.

With all eyes now directed towards the ground, Jim slowly began turning his body towards the buck. Another six inches and he would be in position to shoot.

Suddenly the buck stretched his neck out, laid his horns back, and rushed towards the nearest doe. Jumping in the air, the old doe ran twenty yards straight away from the tree, stopped, and looked back towards the big buck that stopped where the doe had been feeding. Sniffing the ground where she had stood, the buck checked for any sign of the doe coming into estrous. Facing straight away from Jim, he offered no shot though he was only fifteen yards away.

Jim's heart was pounding wildly, his mouth dry from his rapid breathing. If the buck turned broadside the shot would present itself. Jim shifted his gaze from the buck's antlers to the buck's body, trying to calm himself and begin concentrating on making the shot.

The buck remained motionless, staring in the direction of the doe. The doe stared at the buck, her tail held straight out from her body. If she's not in heat, she's real close, Jim thought.

Suddenly the doe's ears perked up and she looked past the buck and behind Jim. The buck turned his head a moment later and instantly laid his ears back flat against his neck. Jim watched as his hair bristled.

Jim knew there was a new visitor on the scene, but he couldn't turn to look, only wait to see what happened next. He didn't have to wait for long.

The woods exploded in the next instant as a huge brown blur of hooves and horns tore past the tree straight for the eight-point. The big eight-point barely had time to turn and lower his head before the monster ten-point cranked into him full bore, driving him backwards until he went end for end off the ridge and disappeared into the brush.

The monster buck turned broadside to Jim, then started back up the ridge toward the startled doe that had run off a short distance further up and away from Jim.

Jim was stunned. The big eight-point had just been banished to the underbrush.

Jim soaked in every detail of the incredible deer. His coat was a shade darker than all the other deer. His face had a grayish color and a dark reddish patch on his forehead. However, it was his immense rack and body size, which mesmerized Jim. The deer's shoulder muscles rippled with each step, his massive neck moved up and down in cadence with his steps. Above it all, was his immense rack. Thick tines reaching up to a foot in length lined his main beams that ended out past his nose. Bleached white by the sun they looked almost unreal as the buck strode to the top of the ridge, stopped and turned broadside.

The buck stood a mere twenty yards away broadside and looked towards the old doe, unaware of Jim slowly bringing his bow to full draw. Terrified that the buck would spot the movement

Jim closed his eyes for a brief moment, thinking somehow this would make him invisible to the deer of his dreams.

The old doe approaching her estrous cycle had brought the magnificent buck into the open. It was this same call of nature's cycle, which now saved him.

As Jim opened his eyes, reaching full draw, he fixed his eyes on the chest of the big body. The old doe picked this moment to move off into the brush to Jim's right. The buck rushed to follow the instant Jim released the arrow.

Jim gasped as the arrow sailed harmlessly over the buck's back and buried itself halfway up the shaft in the carpet of leaves. The buck stopped and looked around quickly, having heard the release of the arrow. His keen senses on full alert now, he quickly moved into the brush where the doe had gone and disappeared without a sound.

Jim leaned his head back against the trunk, closed his eyes and felt his whole body begin to shake along with the oak leaves, gently trembling in the evening breeze.

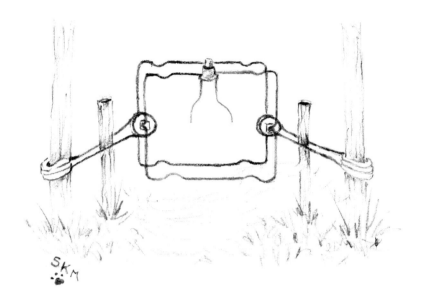

Chapter 12

The smile on Jim's face as he came through the back door told the story to Ann without a word being said.

"You caught another fox!" Ann said as she rolled the sausage sizzling in the frying pan.

"I can't believe it, that makes twelve this week," Jim said as he peeled his jacket off. I've still got Jackson's two fields to check on the way to work. We'd better leave pretty quickly in case I've got to remake any of those sets."

"Wash your hands. You've got time to eat first." Ann finished buttering the toast and loaded two plates. "You should give Ortin a cut of your profits. He sure has gotten you on the right track with your fox line. You make sure you thank him being this is your last day working at the elevator."

Jim slid into the chair and began working over the heaping plate. "With fox over twenty dollars apiece, I've already got over two hundred dollars worth of fur and I've still got a lot of water trapping to do," Jim said between forkfuls of sausage and eggs. "In fact, I'm going to set the first part of Black Creek tomorrow morning. Coon, mink and muskrat season opens today."

"How do you plan on checking all these traps anyway?" Ann said. "And quit eating so fast," she scolded.

"Sorry, Mom," Jim said, reaching for another slice of toast. "The water sets will all be Conibear traps and drowning sets so I can check those after school. Plus, I'm going to pull the fox sets next weekend anyway since deer season opens that Sunday." Jim popped the last bite of sausage in his mouth as he walked to the sink and rinsed off his plate.

"Hurry up with your chores or we'll be late," Ann said glancing at the clock above the stove.

Jim was halfway out the door before Ann finished the sentence. Stepping into his knee-high chore boots in the garage, Jim didn't bother to put on his work jacket. He wouldn't be out that long.

The sows were all in one pen now that their litters were all weaned. They were fed only a small amount twice a day to keep them slim. When it was time to have them bred again, they would produce more pigs if they were a bit on the skinny side.

Jim dumped the half bag to the sows amidst their squealing and pushing. A quick check of the water trough and he was on to the feeder pigs. The sixty-eight pigs were only a couple weeks away from being sold. There was still feed in the two feeders located in the center of the pen.

He would fill the feeder completely with the load of feed they would bring home after work today. The feeder pigs needed a continuous supply of feed to put on as much weight as possible.

The market hogs would also be ready in a couple of weeks, nearing the 210 pounds, which was the goal. The ten hogs had one feeder that was still half-full. Jim jumped the fence and headed back to the house. Chores didn't take long now if the feeders were full and the water was working. He did need to take half a day and clean all the pens. He had better do that today, he thought. Jim kicked off his boots and headed through the back door all in the same motion.

Ann had the truck running when Jim came bouncing out the front door still combing his wet hair. "We can just make it," Jim said, jumping in the passenger side.

"Your last day of work and it'll be the only day you were late," Ann said. She eased the truck onto the road and down the hill crossing over Black Creek.

A large coon waddled into the headlights just before the bridge and disappeared into the ditch as Ann slowed down to avoid hitting it. A smile crossed Jim's face as he thought about the plentiful numbers of coon that ran the banks of the creek.

Ann sped the truck up the hill then slowed again at the top and began looking for the drive into Jackson's hayfield.

"It's just past those two big oaks, Mom," Jim said, leaning forward in his seat, placing both hands on the dash, peering anxiously ahead.

"I've been by here ten thousand times," Ann said. You'd think I could find the driveway by now." She turned the truck left down the lane. To the left, the lane ran a half-mile then turned west and hit the next road that ran north and south. Jackson's old homestead had stood at this point but only the barn remained, stacked to the roof with this year's hay. It was at the point the lane turned south that Jim had placed two fox sets.

A doe and fawn were caught in the headlights as Ann steered around the numerous potholes in the lane. The doe lazily raised her tail and bounded off slowly. The fawn stared at the approaching lights until suddenly realizing that the doe had disappeared, and turned and raced away in the direction Mom had gone.

Suddenly a pair of yellow eyes reflected back towards the truck, and then disappeared. When the eyes reappeared, Jim leaned forward. "We've got another one!" Jim said, hardly able to contain his excitement. "But it almost looks too big for a fox." His eyes were glued on the spot ahead where the eyes would appear and disappear, then reappear again - the animal held fast by the trap.

A small dip in the lane took them out of sight shortly, before topping a small knoll only fifty yards from the trap.

Both Jim and Ann's eyes grew wide as they topped the hill and the animal stood in the headlights of the slowing truck.

"Coyote!" Ann said stopping the truck twenty yards back.

Jim, his mouth still open in disbelief, sat staring at the huge canine. The coyote was a large male caught perfectly across the pad of the right foot. He stared calmly in the headlights, his tail curled between his hind legs.

Jim opened the door and pulled the twenty-two rifle from the case behind the seat. "I don't think I'll have time to remake the set since we still have to check the sets on the other side of the road." Jim opened the bolt on the old single shot and slid in a shell, "My first coyote. I can't wait to tell Dad and show Ortin."

Jim dispatched the coyote and removed him from the trap. The 1.75 Victor Coilspring had done its job. You couldn't even tell which foot he had been held by, unless you looked closely. Jim lifted the coyote into the back of the truck. "He must weigh over thirty pounds," Jim said, returning the rifle to its case.

"That's the first one I've seen up close," Ann said, looking through the window into the bed as she backed up the truck.

Headed back down the lane in the direction they had come, Jim stared intently at the coyote in the back. "I'll have to borrow a stretcher from Ortin. I wonder if there are more around or he was just traveling through."

Ann smiled without answering. She had been around hunting and trapping her whole life. Following her father along his trap-line when she was a little girl, she had even trapped a few muskrats herself and skinned many more. It was still exciting to be around. Living a life with wildlife and livestock playing such a major part of your life kept you a few steps closer to reality and the natural cycles of life and death. This lifestyle actually built a larger respect and admiration for the natural world than others could appreciate.

Ann stopped the truck at the road to check for traffic, knowing full well, there would be none.

Pulling the truck across the road onto the lane on the other side, Ann shook her head. Jim was still talking nonstop. "Ortin says coyotes are a pain to skin. He says you have to flesh them like a coon." Jim finally turned back, facing forward in his seat as they approached the sets on this side of the road.

A frown crossed Ann's brow. "Somebody's been down this lane earlier."

Jim sat up straight, peering ahead. "What do you mean, Mom?"

Ann slowed the truck down to a crawl. "Look there, you can see where someone has gone off the track and the dew is knocked off the hay." Jim nodded his head slowly.

The headlights lost the track as they arched out into the field. "Old man Jackson won't like it that someone was driving across his hayfield," Ann said. Jim's eyes were trained on the lane as the headlights moved along its path.

"Hold it, Mom, there's my sets," Jim said, his voice lacking enthusiasm.

"Looks like somebody else found your sets too," Ann said, slipping the truck into park. The tracks that had left the lane a hundred or so yards back now reappeared at the torn up circle, which had been Jim's set.

Grabbing his flashlight, Jim got out and approached the set. Boot tracks showed in the dew-laden hay approaching from the opposite direction where the other vehicle had parked. The trap was gone and the area had been freshly torn up indicating a catch. Two fresh fox droppings and a small spot of blood told the rest of the story.

The other set a few feet away was undisturbed. Jim walked back towards the truck and climbed in. "Looks like I had a trap and a fox stolen," Jim said, slamming the door shut behind him.

Ann drove towards the end of the lane to turn the truck back around. "Do you think someone knew you had traps set out here or were they out spotlighting deer and saw the fox in your trap?" Ann asked.

Jim looked up from the floor of the truck and sighed. "I think I know who it was."

Jim began telling the story starting with the night he shot the six-point. Ann listened quietly as the truck slowly worked its way back up the lane, the springs squeaking with each hole and bump in the well-worn track.

Chapter 13

Jim looked up at the clock above the office door. Twelve forty-five. Fifteen minutes left of his last day. It was hard to believe the last two months had gone by so fast. The good thing was Stan Porter had promised him the job full time starting next summer after school let out.

Of course that depended on whether or not his mother was still mad at him by then.

It had been a long ride to work this morning. His mother had remained quiet as Jim told the story in its entirety. Then it was Jim's turn to sit and listen.

Ann had told him, in no uncertain terms, that he had no right to keep things to himself like that. "I understand that you were scared and didn't know what to do, but these things affected all of us and at that point it became selfish to keep it to yourself, scared or not," Ann had said as they sat in the parking lot that morning waiting for Mr. Porter. "I'll call Sheriff Raines and see if there is anything that can still be done about the deer being poached. I'm sure you're probably right about Hayes being behind Red being stolen and the fox being taken out of your trap, but there's no evidence unless the tracks can be matched to Jubal's truck. Therefore, we had better not count on getting him for that. Either way, once the sheriff starts questioning him, I'm sure he'll skulk off and not bother us anymore. His type is usually all mouth. He would rather find somebody else to steal from who's not expecting trouble."

    Jim had felt both ashamed and relieved while his mother had spoken. When he stepped from the truck to start work, Jim felt as if a huge weight had been lifted from his shoulders. An uneasy feeling remained deep inside him as he remembered the anger in Jubal Hayes' voice that night in Jackson's hayfield.

    Stan Porter's footsteps on the stairs of the loading dock brought Jim back to reality. "Well, Jim, I can't thank you enough for doing such a great job for me these past couple of months." Stan handed Jim his last paycheck. "No need to punch out today and I put a little extra in your check for your extra effort."

    "Thanks, Mr. Porter," Jim said, slipping the check into his back pocket. "Tell Ortin thanks for all his help."

    Stan pointed toward the far side of the parking lot. "You can tell him yourself, Jim."

    Jim turned to see Ortin's truck parked in front of his mother's truck and the two of them talking. "I'll lock up for you, Jim, and say, if you get that big buck, bring him up here and we'll weigh him." Stan slapped Jim on the back.

    Jim forced a weak smile, jumped down off the dock, and headed towards his mom and Ortin. The big buck was the last thing on his mind. He knew who and what they were talking about. His moment of cowardice was no longer a secret.

    Ortin hadn't worked this morning, as he was now doing the night shift, running the dryers and taking incoming corn from the farmers. Jim hadn't expected to see him at all today, as he wasn't due in for another eight hours.

Ortin stepped out of his truck as Jim approached. "Think you could give me a hand dragging a buck out, Jim?"

"Sure. Is it all right with you, Mom?" Jim searched his mother's face, looking for a clue to her mood.

"We already discussed it, Jim. It's all right with me if you want to." Ann smiled, sending a sense of relief through Jim.

"I'll have him home in a couple of hours, Ann," Ortin said, climbing back into his truck. "I've still got to try and catch a few hours sleep before I head to work tonight."

Jim piled into the passenger side and with a quick wave, the two trucks headed off in opposite directions.

"How big a buck is he?" Jim asked as the truck picked up speed outside of town.

"Well, he's a pretty good one, should go over a hundred inches. He's the eight-point I told you about. I passed up better than a half dozen smaller bucks over the past couple of weeks waiting to get a shot at him." Ortin slowed the truck as they approached Henderson Road. "He's nothing like the buck you're after, but still a good one."

They had only gone about three quarters of a mile off the highway on Henderson Road when Ortin again slowed the truck. Turning left into the driveway of a picked cornfield, he downshifted and steered the truck towards a fencerow that bordered the field, and then drove along it back towards the distant wood line.

"We'll only have to drag him about 300 yards, but I didn't want to take any more time than I had to. I've still got four fox to skin tonight."

Jim turned to look in the back of the truck at Ortin's mention of the fox. "I didn't think to ask if you caught anything today," Jim said as he admired the pile of fox in the back of the truck.

"Your mom said you caught your first coyote this morning. They're quite an animal, aren't they?" Ortin stopped the truck at the edge of the woods and shut the engine off.

"Jim, your mom told me everything that's gone on with

Jubal. I agree with her that, more than likely, he's behind Red's being stolen and the fox this morning. However, I didn't totally agree with her about him just moving on and not bothering you guys anymore once the sheriff questions him. He's had run-ins with the law before and he knows what he can and can't get away with." Ortin pushed his cap back and looked towards the woods for a moment then turned back to Jim. The look of concern on his face made Jim feel uneasy. "I don't want to scare you or your mom, Jim, but he does have a violent side to him. There was an incident a few years back. A fella Jubal had a run-in with a few days earlier got cracked from behind with a bat. They never proved that Jubal did it, because the fella didn't see it coming." Jim nodded and looked down at the floorboard. "He was lucky. A few days in the hospital and they sent him home. Most folks around here all believe Jubal was responsible. I just felt that you both should know that, and if you get into a confrontation with him, just don't turn your back on him, all right?" Jim nodded his head.

"I know now that I should have told Mom right away and maybe none of the rest of this would have happened." Jim's eyes turned back to the floor of the truck. He looked up as Ortin's hand fell across his shoulders.

"Jim, don't browbeat yourself over this. You made a mistake and you learned from it. If you think you're going to reach a point in your life where you never make mistakes, forget it. You'll make mistakes the whole way, hopefully less and less as you go, and you'll get better at correcting them, but they happen from time to time." Ortin smiled and patted Jim again on the back. "Let's go get that buck."

Chapter 14

Ortin gave one last heave and pulled the big buck into the back of his pickup. Both he and Jim were breathing heavily as they had only stopped to rest three or four times the entire 300 yards they had dragged the deer.

Jim was even more impressed with Ortin now. There were times Jim felt as if he were being dragged along as well as the deer. They didn't spend much time picking their way through the underbrush, just straight towards the truck, Ortin's powerful legs churning up the leaves as they plowed along.

Taking a piece of string from his glove box, Ortin wrapped it around the tag on the deer's horns. "I always double up on string around the tag since I had one blow off once while driving down the road."

Jim stood back and admired the buck once again. He had long, white tines with about a sixteen inch spread. The brow tines were five inches long and darker in color except for the tips.

"He's a beautiful buck," Jim said. "I'll bet he weighs 150 pounds dressed." He patted the buck's hindquarters.

"I think you're about right," Ortin said as he slammed the tailgate shut. "Let's get going. I'm going to take him over to Starks' Processing. I don't have time to cut him up myself. I still have another week of working nights, and seven days a week at that. Running all these traps in the mornings and trying to hunt a few hours here and there...." His voice trailed off. Ortin shook his head and smiled. "Some people think I'm a little crazy this time of year, but I wouldn't have it any other way. I've got the rest of the year to sleep."

The two jumped into the cab and started across the field. Jim glanced at Ortin and could see the fatigue on his face. Six hours of sleep a night wasn't much sleep. Especially, when he was on the go, nonstop, for the other eighteen hours a day. It had been almost two weeks, now, that Ortin had been doing this.

"So, Jim, you've got thirteen fox and a coyote so far, not counting the one that was stolen."

"Yeah, but I didn't remake those two sets this morning," Jim said, looking through the back window still admiring the deer.

Ortin pulled out onto Henderson Road and sped towards the highway, obviously in a hurry. "Well, remake your sets and keep them working this whole week. You may still pick up another four or five fox. With all the harvesting going on, there will be some fox starting to look for new areas and you're in good locations to pick them up."

"How many fox have you got altogether?" Jim asked.

"With these four this morning I've got forty and five coyotes. With any luck I should pick up another ten or twelve this week depending on the weather."

Ortin turned his head towards Jim, his voice suddenly serious. "You really need to spend every minute you can spare this week out in the woods. This is the peak of the rut and if you're going to get another chance at the big boy, it's going to be now. He's a record-book buck, Jim, and first place for the

Big Buck contest at the lumberyard is a new shotgun and a free taxidermy mount."

Jim nodded. "I think tomorrow after I check and remake my sets, I'll move both my tree stands to new locations for the last week of the season. I should be able to hunt every evening, plus, we have Friday off from school. Maybe I'll get another chance."

Ortin turned into the driveway leading to Starks' meat processing plant. On the backside of the building was a loading dock next to a loading chute. Ortin backed the truck up to the dock and shut off the engine.

Jim jumped into the back of the pickup while Ortin went in the side door. A moment later, the overhead slid upwards with a loud growl. Alex Starks stood in the doorway. He was every bit the picture of a butcher; his once white apron blood spattered and stretched tightly across his broad stomach. "Nice buck, Ortin. How do you want him cut up?"

Jim grabbed the buck by the horns, pulled him around, and handed the horns over to Ortin and Mr. Starks. With one pull, the two men pulled the deer onto the dock and inside the door.

Ortin tipped his hat back. Jim noticed he always did this when he was thinking. "All the steaks and chops you can get, two sticks of salami, and the rest in burger."

Mr. Starks didn't bother to write the order down; he simply nodded as he busied himself skinning the hide away from the base of the antlers. Once the skin was peeled back, he grabbed a large handsaw and with two quick cuts pulled the antlers free.

Mr. Starks handed the antlers to Ortin. "Most guys would have gotten this one mounted, Ortin."

Ortin held the set of antlers out in front of him. "He's a nice buck all right, but I've already got a couple of others a little bigger mounted. Maybe if I got one as big as what Jim is after I'd get another one mounted."

"Yeah, Jim, what's this I hear about this Monster Buck of Pratt Lake? Have you seen him? Mr. Starks wiped his knife clean on his apron.

"I had a close call a couple of weeks ago. He's big all right, bigger than anything my dad and I have ever seen. I'll be awful lucky to get another chance at him, though."

Ortin jumped down off the dock and laid the antlers in the back next to the four fox. "Give me a call when it's ready, Alex." Ortin opened the truck door.

Mr. Starks reached up with a huge bear-like paw and grasped the rope that connected to the overhead door. "OK, see you later, Ortin, and good luck getting that buck, Jim. I'd sure like to see you pull in here with him." Mr. Starks disappeared behind the door as it groaned its way back down.

Ortin had the truck started before Jim had his door open. "I'll drop you off, head home, skin these fox and can still get almost six hours sleep before I have to be at the elevator by ten." He steered the truck along the drive that circled the entire place.

"I'm going to hustle around and remake my sets before dark, and I still...." The truck came skidding to a halt, cutting Jim off in mid sentence.

Jim turned to Ortin, only to see him staring past Jim out the passenger window. "Look at that." Jim turned to see an old rusted Ford pickup parked in the tall grass with a trailer next to it. The rear of the trailer pointed skyward, the hitch hidden in the tall grass.

"What, that old truck?"

"No, look at the tires on the trailer."

Jim's eyes shifted and grew wide. Each tire was different.

Both Jim and Ortin were suddenly quiet. Ortin broke the silence. "I can't believe that Alex would have had anything to do with stealing that hog. But did you notice who was in the back grinding burger?"

Jim shook his head.

"Trevor Smith," Ortin said, starting the truck forward again. "Do you know who his uncle is?"

Jim craned his neck out the window still staring at the trailer. "Let me guess. Jubal Hayes."

Chapter 15

Jim trotted along the two-track of Jackson's hayfield, his knee boots squeaking noisily. Another hundred yards and he would be at the edge of the woods. He had to come in from this direction. With this new spot, he'd found it was the only way to get to it without walking through all the cover. He was determined to spend as much of the day as possible in this stand.

The past week was a total blur to Jim. He had called Sheriff Raines as soon as Ortin dropped him off Saturday afternoon. It had paid off. Sheriff Raines had called back Sunday night. Trevor had told the sheriff everything after he reminded Trevor that he was a parolee and if he had anything to do with this, it was back to prison. Trevor admitted that the tires matched up to the pictures the sheriff had taken and that Jubal had borrowed the trailer the week Red was stolen.

Trevor had sworn, though, that Jubal hadn't brought Red to the plant and that he knew nothing about any poaching of deer.

Mr. Starks didn't bat an eye. He fired Trevor as soon as he found out and called Ann to apologize for even being remotely linked to what went on. Ann had reassured Mr. Starks that everyone knew his character was not in question.

Sheriff Raines had issued a warrant for Jubal, but he had disappeared, no doubt tipped off by Trevor. Still, Jim and Ann felt it was only a matter of time until they caught him and felt he was no longer a threat to them.

Jim hadn't had much time to think about it, though. Sunday morning Jim had spent cleaning all the barns, while Vic Warner had brought his combine down and harvested the corn behind the house.

Jim made two trips to town with the tractor and wagon hauling corn, and Mr. Warner hauled the rest with his grain truck.

They would store the corn for now and let Ray decide how much to sell to cover expenses and how much to keep in the feed bank.

With only two hours of daylight left that Sunday, Jim had taken off to find a new stand site. He didn't expect to hunt that night, just find a good spot to hunt the rest of the week.

Jim had felt his best chance was to push into cover even deeper. The only problem was disturbing all the deer getting there. That's when he had come up with the idea of circling around and coming in through Jackson's hayfield on the west side.

Jim spotted the trail he had come in on last Sunday. At the edge of the woods, he stopped to catch his breath. Ortin had told him to still hunt his way into his stands. "This way you're a lot less likely to spook deer on your way in, and I've even shot a few from the ground while sneaking into my stands." It was hard to slow down – he had been looking forward to setting this stand all week.

He had found the spot by entering the woods on this same

trail, but when the trail split, one heading up the ridge and the other down into thicker cover, Jim chose to climb the ridge and look from there first.

The top of the ridge was fairly open with huge beech trees forming a canopy that kept any underbrush from growing. Jim could see nearly the entire creek bottom all the way back to the road. The creek itself was only visible in that direction for a few hundred yards before it was swallowed up by the thick growth of willows. It was when Jim looked towards the west end of the lake, that he spotted the tree.

The ridge of hardwoods on the east side of the creek, which separated the creek bottom from the clover at the back of the farm ended where the creek turned east and reached the lake.

It was there that a huge maple stood. The ridge ended seventy-five yards back to the north and the tree was below that point surrounded by switch grass that gave way to the cattails that bordered the lake and now the creek on both sides. The tree was obviously a remnant of days when the ridge had extended farther. It still stood strong and healthy, but looked awkwardly out of place in the open. The tree stood about twenty yards from the creek to the east, and directly across the creek was a dense tangle of willows and briars that had grown thick in open sunlight.

Coming from this side of the creek it was relatively easy to get to. Providing, that you stayed up on the ridge as long as you could before dropping down along the creek at the bend where it swung around the tree.

The creek at this point had a gravel bottom and had widened considerably. The gravel Jim suspected had come from the erosion of the ridge over the years. It was still nearly knee deep, but Jim could cross here with his knee boots if he went slowly.

The tree was perfect for a stand and the deer sign was unbelievable. There were five or six little patches of willow throughout the switch grass, which was shoulder high with trails running in every direction. There weren't any scrapes that he could see, but he hadn't looked around much, not wanting to leave any scent in the area. Two tree steps got him up into the lower branches and from there conveniently spaced branches acted as steps up to about 15 feet where the trunk separated into three smaller trunks. Jim placed the stand just below the spot where the trunk split. From this spot, he could shoot 180 degrees and cover the width of opening, about twenty yards on either side of the tree. It was longer than it had appeared from the ridge. The opening ran for nearly seventy-five yards before the cattails took over.

It had only taken five minutes to put the stand up and he didn't have to cut a single branch for shooting lanes. He could shoot through five separate openings. Any deer passing in front of him would have to pass through one of the openings and eventually offer a shot, providing it was close enough.

Jim reached the edge of the creek. He had crept the whole way in. Ten slow steps, stop, watch and listen. He had repeated this sequence for the last fifteen minutes. Pausing at the water's edge, he took a deep breath and smiled. Everything was perfect. The temperature was in the thirties with a cold, steady breeze blowing straight out of the north. A front was supposed to pass through in few hours and the deer should be moving.

It was nearly 11:00 in the morning. Jim had run all his traps first, then showered, put on clean clothes, packed a sandwich and told his mother not to expect him back until dark. With only two days left before gun season opened, Jim wanted to spend every minute possible at this spot.

Jim slowly waded out into the creek. The gravel bottom and speed of the current formed a sort of mini rapids as the creek widened and then turned sharply towards the lake.

He knew that being quiet was the most important thing now. There were numerous beds in the switch grass surrounding the tree, and for all he knew, the big buck could be bedded there right now.

Reaching the other side, Jim avoided walking in the deer trail that cut into the side of the bank. The deer preferred to cross in this shallow spot also.

He poked his head above the bank and spent a minute just watching the opening. Slowly, pushing the small willow saplings to the side with his free hand, Jim crept to the base of the tree.

After climbing half way up the tree, Jim stopped once again and looked over the scene. Aside from being in a great location, the stand had a beautiful view. Facing east toward the lake it gave him a new perspective of the area. This was a natural funnel. The lake, creek and woods tapering off all came together at this point.

Jim climbed the rest of the way up, fastened the safety harness around his waist and pulled up his bow. Settling back on the seat of his stand, Jim pulled on his facemask and a knit camo hat. He hung his bow on a small hook that he had secured in a branch above his head, putting the bow just off to the side but within easy reach.

The temperature was beginning to fall as the wind picked up slightly. Jim took a deep breath and watched as a snowflake floated down, waving side to side, landed on his knee and slowly disappeared.

Matt Buche

Chapter 16

Jim glanced at his watch, two-thirty, over three hours in the stand. He could wait no longer. Reaching into his coat pocket, he fished out the bologna sandwich wrapped in wax paper. He slowly wadded up the wax paper and shoved it back into his pocket.

He ate with as little movement as possible. He almost wished he had brought his shotgun for all the wood ducks that kept swimming back and forth in the creek. No deer yet, but there were still nearly four hours left of daylight.

Jim finished the sandwich and reached for the water bottle in his pocket. He glanced around slowly to make sure no deer had appeared while his attention was focused on the sandwich-nothing there. Taking one long drink, he emptied half the bottle and returned it to his pocket. There were a few more snowflakes in the air, and Jim thought that if it kept up all night there might be a couple of inches on the ground by morning.

The fox and coyote would be moving, and Jim hoped he would pick up a couple more. He had sixteen fox and two coyotes now. He had caught a female just two days later in the same spot where he caught the big male. The day before yesterday he had caught a double on grey fox back on the clover behind the house. He loved going into the garage and seeing the hides lined up along the wall, stretched, dried and brushed out, all ready to sell.

Ortin had been right about the coyotes. They were no fun to skin. It had taken him almost a half hour to skin each of them.

Even though his catch on fox had dropped off, Ortin encouraged him to keep his sets out. "You'll have more fox move into the area. It may take a week or so, but you'll pick up a few more."

Tomorrow Jim would set out the first part of his water line along Black Creek, starting from the road back towards the lake. He would do that in the morning after checking his fox sets, and then spend the rest of the day back here.

It had gotten noticeably colder in the last fifteen minutes as a dark line of clouds pushed its way southward against the already overcast sky. Jim was glad he'd thrown on an extra set of long underwear and worn his insulated jacket. He had taken great care to make sure everything was clean and ready for this long day on the stand.

Jim watched his breath form a small cloud in front of his face, and then disappeared. It was going to get very cold before this day is over, he thought.

A flight of wood ducks bickering amongst themselves captured his attention for a few moments off to the left as they floated in and around a treetop, which lay halfway into the creek. Finally, the group floated with the current back around the bend and out of sight.

When Jim turned back, he was startled to see a doe facing directly at him from across the opening. She stood frozen like a statue in the middle of the switch grass, the stalks dancing in the wind the only movement. Only her head was showing and Jim wasn't sure if she was lying down or the grass was just that tall.

His question was answered a second later, when a huge rack appeared behind her as the monstrous buck stood up and stretched.

Jim stiffened and felt his mouth go dry. The buck and doe had been lying only seventy-five yards away the whole time. Hidden by the tall grass, they had been as unaware of Jim's presence as he was of theirs.

The buck ignored the doe as she began picking her way through the grass towards Jim. The buck stared north across the creek raising his nose to test the wind time and again.

The doe had moved halfway across the opening before the buck turned and followed. Two low grunts came from the massive buck as he closed the distance to the doe. She glanced back over her shoulder at the sound of the grunts. Her tail, held out parallel to the ground, flicked side to side before she pranced forward another ten yards.

Jim waited until the buck's head went behind a clump of willows and the doe was looking back before he slowly stood and grasped his bow all in one motion.

He suddenly realized that he was not nervous. A feeling of confidence swept through him. The wind was in his favor. He had shot all week long and had never shot better. The broadhead that tipped his arrow was razor sharp - he had spent a half hour working on it last night. Another twenty yards and the buck would be in range. He didn't need to tell himself, in order to stay calm, that he probably wouldn't get a shot. At this point, he knew he would get a shot.

In his mind, the body of the huge buck became the burlap sack hanging between the two posts in the back yard. He no longer let his eyes dwell on the massive horns, but concentrated on finding that small dangling piece of string on the burlap bag to zero in on.

The doe walked within twenty yards of the tree and turned to her right, heading directly for the trail that cut through the bank and across the river. She seemed in a hurry, but the buck would have none of it.

Suddenly, the buck rushed forward, angling through the grass to cut her off from the creek. With his ears laid back tight against his neck, he herded her back away from the creek and towards the tree and Jim.

The buck continued walking towards Jim's left even after the doe had turned back.

The doe deterred, the buck now looked as if he were going to cross the creek.

Jim knew he wouldn't leave the doe. It was obvious from her posturing, that she was in heat.

Jim turned slowly on the balls of his feet and readied himself for the buck to step into his shooting lane.

The buck angled towards the creek, then walked along the edge, starting to circle the doe. Jim stared at the buck's chest; the doe scarcely fifteen yards away directly in front of his stand.

Jim's hand tightened on the bow as the big buck walked into the opening. Jim relaxed his hand, knowing that a tight grip was not what he wanted. His mind was clear and focused, eighteen yards, maybe nineteen. A long shot, but he had practiced from slightly farther.

The buck reached the cut in the bank where the trail crossed and stopped, lowering his head to check for scent. Satisfied he turned his attention back to the doe, taking two steps toward her before stopping broadside.

Jim let his eyes narrow down to a tiny spot in the center of his chest. He felt the strain of his limbs as the bow flexed. The words "follow through" settled in his mind as his index finger reached the corner of his mouth and held for a brief instant. The only motion was the release itself, and Jim held everything in place until he heard the resounding *thwap* of the arrow striking home.

The huge buck gave no indication of being hit. He simply

turned in his tracks and trotted back in the same direction he had come. His tail pressed tight to his body, he slowed to a walk after only twenty yards.

Jim stared at the buck. The last thing he had seen was the white fletching of his arrow disappearing into the massive chest. However, the buck had hardly reacted.

The great buck stopped and lifted his head high and then quickly lowered it again. He took two steps and stumbled, his hind legs faltering. In one motion, he swung towards Jim and collapsed, his hind legs reaching skyward then slowly falling, disappearing into the swaying grass.

Jim looked at the doe still standing beneath the tree, she in turn staring at the spot where the buck disappeared. Jim's knees grew weak and he sat back on the seat and unhooked his safety harness. When he lowered his bow to the ground, the doe caught sight of his motion and with a snort, crashed off into the underbrush to the right.

Shaking, Jim climbed down, collected his bow, and walked to where the buck had stood when he shot. Slowly he walked along the edge of the creek, the sound of his breathing growing heavy as the realization of what happened began to set in. He began walking faster as the blood smeared on the blades of grass grew heavier and more constant. He plowed through a patch of grass as tall as he, his heart pounding, and fell to his knees when he saw the monstrous buck before him.

Jim reached out slowly with his bow and touched the giant. The great buck lay motionless, his eyes blank and lifeless. A wave of sadness overcame Jim and his eyes watered. He knew this sadness and knew that it was only right to feel this way.

But now, that the door had been opened, the tears wouldn't stop. He cried because his father and grandfather were not here to share this with him. He cried because he could see from the past months that he would no longer get to be a little boy. He cried because the cycle of life touches everything, from the death of a deer to the birth of a man.

Matt Buche

Chapter 17

Jim stood staring at the row of fox pelts lined up single file against the far side of the garage. Twenty red fox pelts and two grey fox. The two coyote pelts hung at the end of the garage alongside the fifty muskrat pelts which were all bundled together in groups of ten sorted by size. Two mink pelts still on the stretchers leaned against the far wall on top of the bench, below the fox hides.

It had been quite a season. He still had the twenty coons to put up in the next two weeks before the fur auction. Ortin said he would stop by and show him how to flesh the coon with his new two-handled scraper. For now, the coon were skinned, placed in plastic bags and frozen. He would thaw out five or six the day before Ortin was to come over.

Jim's eyes drifted to the set of antlers on the bench. The skull plate was cleaned and a board had been placed between the two main beams to keep the rack from shrinking. Another month and a half and it could be officially scored for Pope and Young. Ortin had measured the buck and figured it would make both Pope and Young and Boone and Crockett.

"He'll go 175," Ortin had said, shaking his head. "Men hunt their whole lives, Jim, and never even see a buck of this size, let alone get one." Ortin knew that Jim appreciated that buck like no one else would, though, and Ortin bragged about the deer more than anyone did.

Jim knew that he would never have gotten the deer if it hadn't been for Ortin's help and he told people so.

It had been quite a chore dragging the buck out. Ortin and Jim spent nearly an hour getting him out to the edge of Jackson's hayfield. Then it took everything they had to get him into the back of Ortin's truck.

They went right to the elevator and weighed the buck. It wasn't long before a crowd gathered and they had to keep weighing him over and over, because somebody new would walk up and not believe how much it weighed and want to see it weighed again. Two-hundred thirty pounds dressed.

No one had seen anything like this deer before in this area. The rack itself was unbelievable, but it was his huge body that made him almost a freak of nature. It wasn't long before someone from the paper came down with a camera and started snapping pictures. The next thing Jim knew, he was being interviewed for an article. Ortin was smiling and patting Jim on the back the whole while. It had been quite a spectacle.

Ann opened the door into the garage from the kitchen. "I have to run into town and pick up a few things. Did you want me to drop you off at the creek so you can check your traps?"

"Yeah, let me grab my backpack and bow," Jim said.

"What do you need your bow for? You've filled your two tags," Ann said as she slipped on her coat.

"Well, gun season is closed and I've got my small game license so it's legal. All I want to do is target shoot stumps with my blunt."

"Well, as long as it's legal, it's all right with me," Ann said.

Jim set his backpack into the back of the truck and laid his bow next to it. Ann started the truck as Jim jumped in.

It was the first week of December and both Jim and Ann were looking forward to Ray being home in three weeks. They had filled him in on everything with their weekly phone conversations. Ray had been ready to come home when the trouble with Jubal Hayes came out in the open. Ann and Jim had talked him out of it, as no one had seen Hayes since the sheriff had issued the warrant. Rumor had it he was in the U.P. but no one knew for sure.

In the last three weeks since he had shot the buck, Jim had even gotten his picture in the Grand Rapids Press. The new shotgun he had won in the deer contest hung on the wall above his bed. He would have to wait a few months to get his deer mounted as the hide had been sent off to be tanned. Tom Craig, the taxidermist, was anxious to do the head. He had told him it would be the largest deer he had ever mounted.

Ann stopped the truck on the bridge over Black Creek and Jim hopped out, grinning. He grabbed his backpack and bow, waved to his mother and disappeared over the bank.

Jim set his backpack down and peered under the bridge at his first set. The sound of the truck grew faint as Jim stepped under the bridge to see the trap still undisturbed along the edge of the cement culvert.

Jim needed to check only a dozen traps. He had kept out a few coon and mink sets, these being mostly blind sets with a few baited pocket sets. The coon population was very high in the area. In fact, he had taken ten coons alone from the old barn of Jackson's just around the corner. Old man Jackson had called Jim to see if he would trap the coon for him. He had asked Jim to use live traps, though, so he could release any cats he caught. The cats helped keep the mouse population in check. Once again, Ortin had come through with some valuable information. Using marshmallows for bait would attract coon, but the cats would have no interest. It had worked like a charm.

Ten days in a row Jim was greeted by a masked bandit curled up asleep in the live trap.

Jim headed downstream, walking along the creek edge, occasionally picking out a target to shoot at between sets. Set after set was empty, and Jim had already decided he would pull the sets tomorrow when he reached the last set.

A large maple grew alongside the stream about a quarter mile in from the road. The stream had exposed some of the roots and made a tempting maze for any passing mink.

Jim had set a trap on either side of the tangle of roots. Both were staked out in the center of the creek to insure drowning the trapped animal quickly.

Jim swung his pack basket off his back and set it next to the giant maple. Peering around the trunk, he spotted the dark form of a mink floating in the center of the creek. Climbing down the edge of the bank, he used the exposed roots as steps. He held his bow by one limb, reached out and hooked the chain of the trap and pulled it to shore.

When Jim pulled the mink from the water, his jaw dropped. The huge male was nearly thirty inches long from the tip of his nose to the end of his tail. The old buck mink had eluded him for several years. He removed him from the trap, and climbed up to the top of the bank. He wouldn't reset the trap now. Though all Jim had ever seen were his huge tracks in the mud, he felt the familiar sadness welling up in his throat.

Jim placed the mink in the backpack and started back up the creek. He would return tomorrow with his hip boots and pull all the traps. He had taken enough for this year and still left plenty of seed for next.

Jim had only walked about fifty yards back towards the road when he heard the roar of an engine, tires skidding on ground and then voices.

Jim started running. All he could think was that his mother had run into some sort of problem and needed his help. He stayed on the game trail that ran along the top of the creek bank. Running through the brush and undergrowth, he could hear the voices growing nearer but they were men's voices, not his mother's.

Jim stopped and peered ahead through the brush. He was about to yell out when he spotted a form darting through the trees towards him.

Adrenaline shot through him and sent his heart racing as he recognized Jubal Hayes running down the same trail he was on.

Jim knelt down. There were no trees near him, only the steep creek bank to his right. He thought about diving over the edge, but Jubal suddenly ducked behind a tree and peered back in the direction he had come. It was then that Jim saw the double-barreled shotgun in his hand.

"Hayes, give it up, there's no way out." It was Sheriff Raines and Jim could tell he was not far behind Hayes.

Jim saw Jubal Hayes slowly bring the shotgun to his shoulder just as Sheriff Raines came into view on the trail about sixty yards away.

There was not time to think. "Look out!" Jim screamed as he drew his bow. He didn't remember grabbing the arrow.

Jubal Hayes turned, swinging the muzzle of the shotgun towards Jim, his face red, the yellow teeth showing as his lips coiled into a twisted smile.

Jim focused on the evil face, released the arrow and dove backwards.

Jim heard the shotgun blast and the buckshot whistling as he fell as if in slow motion. The clouds moving above the leafless branches disappeared as the swirling, frigid water of Black Creek pulled him under.

Matt Buche

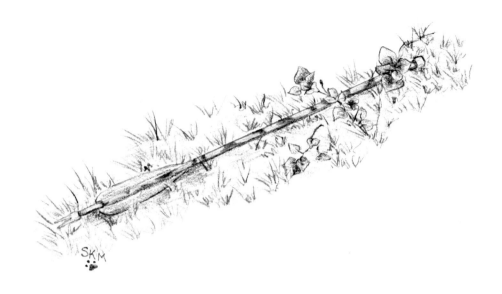

Chapter 18

"Jim! Jim! Are you all right?" Ortin's strong hands pulled Jim free from the water and laid him on the bank.

"I think so," Jim said, finally catching his breath. He tried to sit up.

"Hitting the water must have knocked the wind out of you," Ortin said. He helped Jim to his feet.

They climbed up the bank and walked towards the sheriff, who stood over Jubal Hayes.

Jubal Hayes rolled into a sitting position, his hands cuffed behind his back. He lifted his face to Jim and Ortin, and Jim winced at the sight.

Both of Jubal's eyes were swollen, with a golf ball sized welt, perfectly round, centered on his forehead. Blood trickled from both nostrils.

"Nice shot, Jim," Sheriff Raines said. He handed Jim his

arrow tipped with the rubber blunt. "Come on, Hayes." The sheriff pulled Jubal to his feet and pushed him forward on the trail back towards the road.

"What happened, Ortin? How did Jubal end up here with you and the sheriff chasing him?"

"The sheriff got a tip Hayes was back in town last night. We were on our way out here to warn you and your mom when we met her around the corner. While the sheriff was explaining everything to her, I spotted something coming out from behind Jackson's old barn headed down the two-track towards your road. I put the binoculars on it and, sure enough, it was Jubal's truck."

Jim shouldered his backpack. "Did he go to our place?" Jim asked.

"Yes," Ortin answered. "We knew from your mom that you were back in the woods, so we waited where the two-track crosses your road so he had no way out." Ortin looked at Jim. "We met him right on the bridge when we saw him coming and that's when he took off through the brush."

The two walked behind the sheriff and Hayes along the trail. Ortin pushed his hat back. "I think he thought you were still working at the elevator. Waited for you and your mom to leave this morning, and then made his move."

Jim stopped, shivering now from his wet clothes. "What did he take?"

Ortin sighed. "He had all your furs and the rack, Jim." He placed his hand on Jim's shoulder.

"He's done now, though. He won't see the light of day after taking that shot at you."

Jim could only nod as they walked slowly up the trail towards the road.

Chapter 19

The red barn, washed in the morning sun and covered with the pelts from Jim's trap line, made quite a sight.

"Mom, did you find the camera yet?" Jim asked. He climbed down from the stepladder after hanging the last pelt.

Ann stood on the porch. "Yes if I can just remember how to use it."

Ortin smiled. Don't forget to get your racks in the picture, too. Your grandkids will want proof after you're done telling this story."

Ann came down off the porch and headed towards the barn. "Let's get these taken so you two can get going to your auction."

"You'll be glad you took these pictures, Ann," Ortin said quietly as Ann snapped several pictures from different angles. "A few more years and he'll be off to college."

Ann turned slowly to Ortin. "I want to thank you for all that you've done for Jim, for us." She looked down, tears welling.

Ortin smiled and started to answer, but was cut off by the sound of a vehicle coming down the road.

They all recognized Max Logan's truck, as well as his passenger.

Jim ran towards the truck, the rack of the monster buck still in his hand. He met his dad as he stepped out of the truck and had him in his arms before he could say anything. Jim buried his face in his dad's shoulder and fought back the tears. "I missed you, son," Ray whispered. Jim gave no response but to hold his father tighter.

"I was hoping you two would hurry up and get here. I didn't know how much longer I could stall them," Ann said, waiting her turn.

Jim pulled away, his eyes wet, a smile on his face. "You knew?"

"It was your dad's idea to surprise you," Ann said. She stepped between them and hugged Ray tightly.

"Well, I hate to run off," Max Logan said, "but I've got to get to town."

"Thanks again, Max," Ray said. They all waved as Max's truck headed out the drive.

Ray shivered, "It's a little colder than in Florida. Let me grab my winter coat and we can take off."

"That's why you brought your car, Ortin!" Jim said. "You knew too?"

Ortin pushed his cap back and smiled, "Yeah, I was in on it."

"You're going too, aren't you, Mom?" Jim asked.

"Of course, someone's got to keep an eye on you boys," Ann said.

Jim watched as his mother fixed the collar on his father's coat. Ortin started taking down the pelts and tying them in bundles.

Jim glanced down at the massive rack of horns, and then turned as three geese swept past the barn honking loudly, heading towards the last patch of open water in the center of the lake.

Epilogue

    The big eight-point lay deep in the tangle of cattails, his bed, the remnants of an abandoned muskrat house.
    Just as he had been once kept out, he tolerated no other buck. There was no conscious thought to keep others out. It was survival, pure and simple.
    He had survived the hunting season, passed on his genes to several does, and now would spend his time feeding at night to put on as much fat as possible before the coming winter. His days were spent tucked away here where no predator, either four legged or two, could approach unnoticed.
    The buck licked his nose and raised his head, testing the breeze. His ears shot forward on alert, then, relaxed, as the familiar honking of geese grew nearer.

Matt Buche